## Praise for *Past the Shallows*

'A work by a new master. Like Winton's *That Eye, The Sky*, Parrett's debut is an uncompromising and memorable tale' *Sunday Tasmanian*

'Parrett's debut marks the addition of a strong voice to the chorus of Australian literature' *Canberra Times*

'Finely crafted . . . genuinely moving and full of heart' *Age*

'A fresh and vital voice in Australian fiction' *Australian Women's Weekly*

'A small gem of a story' *Who Weekly*

'A rare work of fiction' *Good Reading*

'An amazing book by a wonderful writer – Cormac McCarthy meets David Vann meets Favel Parrett. Read this book' *Sunday Times*

'Clearly the work of a talented new novelist' *Weekend Australian*

'Her prose is as powerful as a rip' WISH Magazine, *Australian*

'Wintonesque' *Herald Sun*

'Compared to the likes of Tim Winton and Andrew McGahan' *Illawarra Mercury*

D1078731

# PAST THE SHALLOWS

## Favel Parrett

JOHN MURRAY

First published in Australia and New Zealand in 2011 by Hachette Australia

First published in Great Britain in 2012 by John Murray (Publishers)
An Hachette UK Company

1

*Past the Shallows* has been written with the encouragement of Queensland
Writers Centre (QWC). Favel Parrett participated in the 2008 QWC/Hachette
Australia Manuscript Development Program, which received funding from the
Queensland Government through Arts Queensland.

This project has also been greatly assisted by the Australian
Society of Authors (ASA) through its mentorship program;
and the Copyright Agency Limited (CAL) with its support
of the ASA mentorship program through its Cultural Fund.

A CIP catalogue record for this title is available from the British Library

ISBN 978-1-84854-750-6
Ebook ISBN 978-1-84854-751-3

Printed and bound by Clays Ltd, St Ives plc

*To Linda – for always listening*

*It would be vain of me to attempt to describe my feelings when I beheld this lonely harbour lying at the world's end, separated as it were from the rest of the universe — 'twas nature and nature in her wildest mood . . .*

ADMIRAL D'ENTRECASTEAUX, 1792

*O*ut past the shallows, past the sandy-bottomed bays, comes the dark water – black and cold and roaring. Rolling out the invisible paths. The ancient paths to Bruny, or down south along the silent cliffs, the paths out deep to the bird islands that stand tall between nothing but water and sky.

Wherever rock comes out of deep water, wherever reef rises up, there is abalone. Black-lipped soft bodies protected by shell.

Treasure.

*H*arry stood on the sand and looked down the wide, curved beach of Cloudy Bay. Everything was clean and golden and crisp, the sky almost violet with the winter light, and he wished that he wasn't afraid. They were leaving him again, his brothers, Miles already half in his wetsuit and Joe standing tall, eyes lost to the water.

Water that was always there. Always everywhere. The sound and the smell and the cold waves making Harry different. And it wasn't just because he was the youngest. He knew the way he felt about the ocean would never leave him now. It would be there always, right inside him.

That was just how it was.

'What should I find?' he asked.

Joe shook his dry wetsuit out hard. 'Um . . . A cuttlefish bone, a nice bit of driftwood . . .'

'A shark egg,' Miles said.

And there was silence.

Harry waited for Miles to say he was joking, waited for him to say something, but he didn't. He just kept waxing his board.

So Harry stood up and ran.

He followed the marks of high tide left behind on the sand and his eyes skimmed the pebbles, the shiny jelly sacks, the broken shells. Cuttlefish were easy but shark eggs were impossible. They looked just like seaweed. He kept thinking he'd found one only to realise it was just a bit of kelp or a grimy pebble. There was hardly any point trying. But he did try. He always found everything on the list. Always.

There was a cormorant gliding low, its soft white stomach almost touching the water, and Harry watched it as it moved. He watched it slow down and land on a rock on the shore. He walked close, walked right up to the rock, but the bird didn't move. It just stayed still. And he'd never seen one alone. Not like this, on the land. They were always in groups, cormorants. Huddled together in groups on the cliffs and rocks, long necks reaching up to the sun. Sometimes they stayed like that all day. Together. Waiting and watching. Resting.

The bird called softly, and Harry was so close that he felt the sound vibrate inside him. He wanted to reach out and touch it, to stroke the silky shimmering feathers down the cormorant's back. But he stayed still, kept his arms by his sides. He thought that maybe the cormorant was sick. That maybe it couldn't find the others. And he didn't know how they made it, how they survived. Flying over all that ocean, flying and flying in the wind and in the rain. Diving into the cold water.

They washed up in the surf sometimes, the lost ones.

The bird called again. It bobbed its head up and down and spread its wings, then it was gone.

Harry left the beach and ventured into the dunes. Might find a good bit of driftwood in there or something interesting at least. He ran up and down the small humps and valleys, the loose sand getting firmer under his feet, and he kept on going. He could hardly see the beach anymore. It was further than he had ever been. He slowed down, started walking. He looked ahead. There was some kind of clearing, small trees all around. Shrubs. It was a good sheltered place, the wind wouldn't get in this far even if it was really blowing. You could camp here. You could stay here and it would be all right.

Behind a shrub, a pile of shells. A giant pile – old and brittle and white from the sun. Oyster and mussel, pipi and clam, the armour of a giant crab. Harry picked up an abalone shell, the edges loose and dusty in his hands. And every cell in his body stopped. Felt it. This place. Felt the people who had been here before, breathing and standing alive where he stood. People who were long dead now. Long gone. And Harry understood, right down in his guts, that time ran on forever and that one day he would die.

The skin on his hands tingled and pricked.

He dropped the shell and ran.


He had to wait for ages but finally Joe came in. Miles stayed out. He was way out deep and it didn't even look like there were any waves out there. He was just sitting in the water. Just sitting there and Harry was starving, couldn't stop thinking about those sandwiches. The cheese and chutney ones.

'I didn't find it. The shark egg.'

Joe was struggling with his wetsuit, getting his arms free and he was twisting and panting, not looking at Harry. 'Maybe next time,' he said, but Harry didn't think it was likely.

When Joe was finally back in his clothes he started unpacking the stuff from the dinghy, the thermos and the tin cups and the rug and the sandwiches. As long as they didn't have to wait for Miles – no, Harry wouldn't be able to wait for Miles even if Joe said he had to because Miles could stay out in the water forever, even if it was freezing, and Harry just had to have one of the sandwiches now.

'This place is old,' he said, his mouth full of bread.

Joe made a sound but he wasn't really listening. He was somewhere else, maybe still out there in the water with Miles. But it didn't matter.

This place was old. Harry knew it.

As old as the world.

*M*iles got in the dinghy with the men, with Martin and Jeff and Dad, and he didn't speak. No one spoke on the way out to the boat. He hadn't been able to eat his toast at home in the early darkness, and now just on dawn he wished he had.

His stomach was empty, this first day.

First day of school holidays. First day he must man the boat alone while the men go down. Old enough now, he must take his place. Just like his brother before him, he must fill the gap Uncle Nick left.

Because the bank owned the boat now. Because the bank owned everything.

The boat chugged and rattled its way through the heads, and Miles felt the channel grab hold, pull on her hard. She was weak, the *Lady Ida*, she seemed old now, and the crossing was slow. She ploughed through the deepest part of the channel leaving a wide wake of ridges behind, and Miles knew this was where it would have happened. Where Uncle Nick would have been dragged out alone in the dark where the rip ran strongest.

And they never found him.

Not one bit.

Not his beanie.

Not his boots.

Not his bones.

Just the dinghy floating loose, empty and washed clean.

Nobody talked about it now, but back then Dad talked about it. He said Uncle Nick must have gone out to check the mooring. He said he'd never forgive himself.

The boat was almost new, anchored out at the mouth of the bay because the swell was right up – a big winter swell, and all the boats were out there. But Nick wouldn't leave it alone. He wouldn't stop worrying about the boat. Dad said he went on and on about it at the pub and in the end Dad told him to go and check the damn thing. To go and check it or just shut up about it.

And Miles knew exactly how dark it was that night, the sky blacked out by cloud so thick that nothing came through – no stars or moon or anything. Uncle Nick wouldn't have been able to see the dinghy or the land or even his own hand in front of his face.

And everyone forgot about him out there because that was the night of the crash.

That was the night when everything changed.

Martin touched his shoulder, stood close.

'It'll be all right,' he said.

Dad and Jeff were in the cabin and Jeff was staring at him again so Miles looked away. He slipped his yellow windcheater over his jumper. Dad didn't have any small enough for him, so he had to wear a man's size and it was baggy, hung way down past his hands. It was almost better not to wear one at all. He'd get soaked anyway. The only part of him that would stay warm was his head under the tight wool beanie that made his scalp itch.

He rolled up the sleeves, he put on his gloves.

Bruny was coming clear in the new light.

Miles watched the surface change colour – come to life. And even though they were still out deep, away from land, there were places where the water rose like it was climbing a hill, places where the water was angry. And it wasn't the back of a wave. It wasn't a peak in the swell. It was the current surging into rocks that hid below, rocks that you couldn't see even when the tide was low. And if you didn't know what the rise in water meant, you would never guess those rocks were there. The Hazards. They were called the Hazards of Bruny.

They were all around here, out deep. Rocks that weren't attached to land but were big enough on their own to disturb the water – to change its path. And maybe they had been islands once, those rocks. Small islands or maybe even bigger ones before they got worn away. Worn by the water and by the wind and the rain until they were gone from sight. And only the foundations remained, hidden and lost under the sea.

There were things that no one could teach you – things about the water. You just knew them or you didn't and no one could tell you how to read it. How to feel it.

Miles knew the water. He could feel it. And he knew not to trust it.

*T*he air was cold and the house was quiet. Harry got out of bed and shoved his bare feet into his sneakers. Out in the kitchen, if he stood right on the tips of his sneakers, he could just reach the peanut butter jar up in the top cupboard. He ran his finger around the inside of the almost empty jar. There was only enough peanut butter for one slice, so he put two pieces of bread in the toaster and made a toast sandwich.

Even though the embers were dead, Harry sat down by the wood heater to eat. He ate quickly. Aunty Jean would be here soon to take him to the Regatta and he'd better get dressed properly. He'd better find the scarf she'd made him and wear it. He'd better put on the navy blue parka she'd bought him for Christmas. He didn't really like the parka because it was too big and he didn't like the colour, but it was warm. Anyway, he didn't have another coat. Only a thin rain jacket.

He wished Joe would take him to the show instead of Aunty Jean, but at least she didn't talk much in the car. She had the radio on, but it was mostly a man talking and not enough songs. Harry tried to listen to the talking so that he didn't have to think about the road. It was a long drive and the worst bit was still to come. The bit where the thin little road curved around and around as it climbed up the back of Mount Wellington. That was where his ears usually popped and where he usually got carsick.

He tried hard not to get carsick. Aunty Jean might turn back and take him home if he got sick. He kept his eyes on things inside the car. He looked at the dash and down at his legs. He looked at the black mat that his feet rested on. He looked at Aunty Jean's white lumpy hands wrapped tight around the steering wheel.

Finally, they were at Fern Tree. Harry opened and closed his jaw a few times to help his ears clear. He thought about asking Aunty Jean to stop so he could go to the toilet, but he decided to hold on. They were finally on the other side, going down. He could look out the window and see Hobart in slivers through the trees that lined the road. Parts of houses and bits of roads, flashes of blue water and white sails. And as the trees thinned out, there were more and more houses. The city finally came into view as a whole and Harry loved it. All the buildings and the cars and all the things to do.

Aunty Jean parked the car on the grass near the cenotaph. She wanted to see the wood chopping and it started at eleven. That meant they had forty minutes, so after finding the portable loos, Harry led them straight to the rides.

He wanted to take his time, look at them all because he knew he would only be allowed to go on one. Some of the rides looked scary and some were boring, like the merry-go-round. The Gee-Whizzer looked the best, but he needed Miles here to go on it with him. If he went by himself he would slide along the seat every time the ride spun in a new direction. There was no way he could get Aunty Jean on the Gee-Whizzer. Maybe she'd go on the ferris wheel.

As they walked around, Harry noticed all the game stalls; the moving clown faces, darts, hoops, and one he didn't know. There were lots of jars arranged on a table, and some had money in them. Notes. The jar in the middle had a ten-dollar note in it. You had to throw a one-cent piece into a jar containing a note and, if you did, you won the money.

'Maybe I could have a go at that?' he said.

Aunty Jean looked over at the stall.

'Nobody ever wins those games, Harry. They're set up so that no one wins. If you spend the money I give you there, you won't be able to go on a ride.'

Harry looked over at the Gee-Whizzer one more time. Kids were screaming their heads off as the carriages twirled. 'I don't think I want to go on a ride,' he said.

'Well, don't be disappointed when you don't win anything.'

Harry took the dollar note from her hand and ran over to the stall. A hairy, red-eyed man gave him three one-cent pieces to throw at the jars. He threw the first way too far and it missed the table altogether. It landed on the grass. Harry thought that maybe it didn't count and he could start again, but the man shook his head. It counted.

He threw the second and it hit the rim of an empty jar and then fell onto the table. Harry threw the last coin more carefully. And it worked. The coin bounced off the rim of one jar and landed in another that had a five-dollar note in it.

'I won! Aunty Jean, I won!'

'No, you didn't. It doesn't count.' The bearded man pointed to a large sign that had a lot of black writing on it. 'The coin must go straight in. It can't bounce off another jar first.'

Aunty Jean was suddenly right beside him.

'Come away, Harry. I told you it was a waste of money.'

Harry felt his face getting hot. People were looking over and he kept his eyes down as he walked away from the stall. Aunty Jean kept on talking, going on about how he'd wasted his money and Harry stopped listening. He studied people's feet as they walked. He looked at all the shoes that passed by. There were lots of gumboots. There were lots of strollers and prams, and even though it was only the first day of the Regatta the grass had already been worn away where people walked. The dark sticky earth was covered in wrappers and plastic bags and squashed hot chip buckets. Then Harry saw it. Twenty bucks. It was just lying there and a woman trod right on it, and she didn't notice it. She just kept on walking.

Harry dropped down and grabbed it. It was crumpled and muddy but it really was twenty bucks. It really was.

Aunty Jean stopped walking. She looked down.

'Don't sulk, Harry. It doesn't suit you.'

Harry held the note up, 'Look!'

Aunty Jean huddled over him. 'Get up and put it in your pocket before someone says they dropped it.'

Harry stood up, shoved the note in his pocket and he kept his hand on it so it wouldn't fall out. It was his now. He wasn't going to lose it.

'It's a lot of money, Harry. A lot of money. You can buy your own show bags now, OK? But don't spend it all. You should save it. Save it,' she said.

But Harry was way ahead of her. Now he could get two show bags and one for Miles and go on a ride, and maybe get a show bag for his friend Stuart because Stuart never got to come to the show, and when Ben at school busted Harry's He-Man's head off, Stuart let him play with his He-Man. Stuart had He-Man and Battle Cat and Beast Man and Skeletor. Harry should probably buy him a He-Man show bag.

Aunty Jean was looking at her watch. Harry knew her legs would be hurting by now and that she wanted to get off to the wood chopping, but he didn't care. He had twenty bucks. He could get whatever he wanted and Aunty Jean couldn't say anything about it. He could get ten show bags if he wanted. Ten!

'We'd better go and get a seat. Brian Roberts's boy is competing. Heath? Is that his name?'

Harry nodded.

Inside the marquee they sat on plastic seats near the front. It was crowded and the competitors in their white t-shirts were already standing on the centre stage of grass, checking their equipment. Harry recognised Heath Roberts. He was the skinniest man up there, but he had the most hair – thick blond hair just like his brother Justin. Justin had been in Miles's year at school.

The first four men took their positions on top of the huge logs. The starter gun fired, and four sharp metal axes swung through the air. Wood chips went flying and the metal swung and swung. It was making Harry hot, all the movement and noise, all the metal slicing into wood. And it wouldn't stop, the hack, hack, hack. And the crowd were grunting and yelling and a man next to him kept screaming, 'Come on, boy, come on!'

Harry tugged on Aunty Jean's coat sleeve.

'What is it?' she said, but she didn't move her eyes. They stayed with the axes, stayed fixed on the men.

Harry tugged harder. 'I feel sick,' he said.

'Damn! Heath's out.'

The metal noise stopped, and the crowd clapped and cheered. Harry looked over and a big bald man with a sweaty head had busted through his log. It lay on the grass in two pointy pieces.

'I feel sick,' Harry said again.

Aunty Jean looked at him now. 'Yes, you do look pale. Go and get some fresh air and come and get me if you need me. I want to see the final.'

She turned her attention back to the action and Harry pushed his way through to the exit before the next heat started. Out in the light, away from the noise and crowd, he started to feel better. He could breathe again. He could think about the show bags.

Cadbury's bags were the best. They had the most chocolate, but they were pricey. Four bucks. He bought one for Miles, and one for himself, and he looked at the He-Man bag. It was OK, with a face mask, colouring book and a plastic belt, but he decided it was probably better to get Stuart a lolly bag. He got a Redskins bag because it had stacks of Redskins, Choo-Choos and Toffee Apples. He got one for himself, too, and a Bertie Beetle bag because it was cheap and came with a cowboy hat and an orange dart gun. Then he bought two hot American donuts and a can of lemonade.

He had $4.50 left.

He sat down on a patch of grass that overlooked the water. The Tasman Bridge was a giant concrete frame and underneath it the Regatta was all going on. Rowing races, sail boats, larger ferries patrolling up and down with large colourful flags. Harry ate the donuts and felt good. Miles would love the Cadbury's bag. He could give him a Redskin or a Toffee Apple, too, if he wanted.

He saw one of the animal sheds and decided to go in. He wanted to make sure the chopping was over before he went back to Aunty Jean. Inside it was warm and smelled like manure. A huge bull gave him the evil eye as he scooted by. Harry didn't care what people said about cows being dumb. He knew they were smart by the way they looked at you. They were just waiting to get you as soon as you turned your back.

In the next aisle there were goats – white ones, brown ones, and a strange looking black and tan one with big ears. There were four babies with it and above the pen was a blue ribbon that said 'Best In Show 1983'. Harry squatted down and stuck his hand through the bars. One of the babies ran over and tried to bite his thumb. It didn't seem to have any teeth, so it didn't hurt. After a few bites, it gave up and started rubbing the top of its head against Harry's arm.

'They're real beauties, aren't they?'

Harry shot up. A tall man wearing overalls was standing right behind him.

'I'm sorry,' Harry said, and the baby goat bleated. It looked up to see where its scratching post had gone.

'You're all right, son,' the man said. He had a lined, smiling face. He bent down and picked the little goat up.

'Here – you can hold it if you like. It's an African goat. It's called an Anglo-Nubian.'

Harry looked at the goat. It had started chewing the man's overalls. He wanted to hold it. He wanted to climb in the pen and sit down and play with all the goats. Like the time with Mum, when they had come to the show and they had all sat down in the straw and a little goat came up and licked Harry's face and its tongue was hard and rough, but its breath was warm on his cheek and it let out a little bleat right in Harry's ear. Harry bleated back and it had made Mum laugh. 'I love goats,' she'd said.

'My aunt's waiting,' Harry said.

The man nodded and he smiled. He put the little goat back in the pen with the others and Harry ran out of the shed holding his show bags tight as he wove his way through families and packs of screaming teenage girls.

~

'Looks like somebody did well,' Aunty Jean said, looking down at the show bags Harry carried in both hands.

'They're not all for me.'

'Well, just don't eat too many lollies now. We'll have a bit more of a look around and then we'll go into town for lunch. They only seem to have dagwood dogs and chips here.'

Harry decided not to tell Aunty Jean about the donuts and lemonade.

'I can buy lunch.' Harry pulled out the crumpled notes and coins he'd stuffed in his pocket and put them on the table.

'Oh, Harry.' Aunty Jean's eyes closed for a second. 'You're so much like your mum.'

She went to touch his head, but her hand only got part of the way before she pulled it back. Harry stared at the last toasted sandwich triangle on the table. It was cheese and ham.

'Go on, you have it,' she said.

Harry grabbed it and started eating. He tried not to look at Aunty Jean because he knew she was crying. She wiped her face with a hankie and took a big breath.

'Tea always makes things better, doesn't it?' She poured some into her cup and added milk.

Harry nodded.

'We'll do a big shop at the supermarket before we leave town, but I want to get back before dark, so we'll be quick.'

'Can we get peanut butter?' Harry asked.

Aunty Jean closed her eyes again and Harry pushed his chair away from the table and stood up.

'I'm just going to the toilet,' he said.

He took his time, washing his hands twice and drying them carefully with the paper towel. When he opened the door that led into the café, he saw that Aunty Jean was back to normal. She smiled at him when he sat down.

The trip home went by quickly. The sun was on its way down, but there was still enough light for Harry to inspect his show bags, piece by piece. He wondered what Miles would choose to eat first. Whatever it was, he'd choose the same.

'Thanks!' Harry said, and he meant it.

Aunty Jean nodded and smiled. She unloaded the shopping but left the bags by the front door.

'Get your brother to give you a hand. I won't stop in.'

This wasn't unusual if Dad was home. Aunty Jean and Dad didn't speak anymore, not since she made

Dad buy Uncle Nick's share of the boat and he had
to get another loan.

'Here.' She put his smaller show bags inside the
Cadbury's bags so it looked like he only had two.
'Best not show off. Give Miles the rest of the money
to look after.'

Harry was desperate to get inside in case she
started crying again, but he waited until she got back
in the car. He waved, then opened the front door.

Dad was on the couch watching TV.

'We got some shopping, Dad. It's all here.'

Dad barely looked over, but nodded.

'Miles and I will unpack it.'

Harry ran through the lounge carrying the show
bags. Miles was lying on his bed, staring at the
ceiling.

'Miles! I got you a show bag!'

'Sh! Dad's got a headache.'

Harry shut the door. He tried to talk quietly.

'I found twenty bucks! I got you a Cadbury's bag.
*A Cadbury's bag!*' Harry held the purple bag up higher
so that Miles could see it properly. 'I got Stuart a
Redskins bag and I got a Cadbury's bag, too, and
a Redskins and a Bertie Beetle. You can share if you
want. There's a dart gun game. We can play it later.'

Harry noticed that Miles was holding his hands strangely. They were red and swollen. They looked bad.

'Did you hurt your hands on the boat?'

Miles sat up slowly. 'I just gotta wait for the blisters to heal up, that's all.'

'You could put fish cream on 'em?'

'Maybe later.'

Miles went to lie back down but Harry stopped him.

'We've got to unpack the shopping. It's at the door. I'll carry the bags, you can put the stuff away. We got six bags – we got everything! Cup-a-soups, macaroni, Milo, peanut butter.' Harry dumped the show bags on the bed and headed back to the door, hoping Miles would follow.

They unpacked quickly, without talking. Harry grinned when he handed Miles a family-sized packet of Teddy Bear biscuits.

'Another beer, Dad?' Miles asked.

He nodded, and Miles took over a can from the fridge.

Harry walked back to the bedroom and started arranging his chocolate and lollies on the floor.

'What are you gonna have first?' he asked, when Miles came in.

Miles just shrugged.

'I think I'm going to eat the plain Freddo and one Redskin. Then I'll choose two things tomorrow.'

'Maybe you should just eat what you want now.' Miles sat on his bed and looked at the pile. 'What are you saving it all for anyway?'

Harry put all the sweets back in their bags, except for the Freddo.

'If I save them they'll last longer – they'll last until school,' he said.

He looked up at Miles.

'Aren't you going to have any of yours?'

'I'm just tired.' Miles lay back down on the bed again. 'You're lucky you get seasick, Harry. You won't ever have to work on the boat.'

Harry sat on the floor and took small, quiet bites of his chocolate frog.

*M*iles kept his eyes on the water and listened to the engine. He listened to the *chug-chug* and the air pump's whirling churn. As long as it kept pumping, as long as he sorted in time, as long as he steered the boat carefully, everything would be OK. But out at the Friars, steep and black, seals watched the boat from the rocks where they lay in piles half asleep. The cliffs behind were like giant guardians standing tall.

And God, it felt like some kind of ancient place.

The water sucked and moved, smashed against the rocks, and no matter how Miles positioned the boat, no matter how hard he tried, he couldn't keep a clear fix on the airlines. He wiped the sea spray off his face, checked the air pump one more time, and he thought about going into the cabin for a minute to thaw out. To get out of the wind. But he saw something on the water. A catch bag.

It broke the surface, inflatable buoys pulling it up from deep, and Miles edged the boat closer. He hooked the bag with a long metal rod and dragged it around to the back where the boat was flat and low. With his hands on the netting he leaned back and used his body weight to get the abalone up on deck. Yesterday he had fallen backwards when the bags lurched out of the water, but not this time. This bag was light, not even half full.

Inside, the abs stuck fast to each other and formed one giant rock. Miles used the blunt metal blade to separate them out. He sorted them by size and put them in the plastic tubs. Most of them were small, undersize, but Miles knew better than to throw them back. Dad would kill him. The cannery turned a blind eye to these things. They never asked questions. Not of Dad, anyway.

When the bag was empty, Miles checked over the abs. Most of them had stuck to each other again, piled high in the corners of the blue plastic tubs. He reached into the water and picked one up, held it upside down. The black slimy disc of flesh flinched against the cold air. And it was strong, that muscle.

If you put it against your skin, it would grab on, suck hard. It was the only defence it had.

He used to feel sorry for the abs when he was young. The way they pulsed and moved in the tubs, sensing the bright light and heat. But he couldn't think about them like that now. He was only careful not to cut or bruise them, because once abs started to bleed, they kept on bleeding until all the liquid inside them was gone. They just dried up and died.

Miles looked up as Martin's bald head appeared in the water. He dropped the abalone back in its tub, watched Martin pull himself up on deck and sit on the back of the boat. He was such a big man, just a thick, wide back and a thick, wide neck. And he never wore a hood, so his skin was always red from the cold. But he wasn't like he looked. He wasn't like Dad.

He took his mask and mouthpiece off but he didn't speak. He was just breathing. Taking big breaths in and out with his head down. Miles stood behind him for a moment and waited. He went to get the bag Martin had brought up with him out of the water, but Martin stood up and stopped him.

'I'm the one being paid,' he said, and he winked.

Miles stood back, watched Martin work. He watched his hands – so quick and careful. And even when his bloodshot eyes looked out at the water, his hands never stopped moving. The tool never slipped, his hands never hesitated. They just separated and sorted smoothly until the bag was empty. Then he put the shucking knife down, walked into the cabin and poured some tea out of the thermos. He handed Miles a cup.

'They'll be up soon,' he said.

Miles took his gloves off and held the warm cup against his bare hands. The sun was high now and the water had changed from black to deep blue, and the white water churned up against the rocks was so bright against the sky that it was almost blinding. It must be at least ten, maybe even eleven already.

There was a seal resting in the swell, its head and neck reaching out of the water, and Miles could see its black eyes, its long whiskers. It looked right at the boat, right at Miles, and sniffed the air like it knew exactly what had been taken. What was on board. It opened its mouth, let out a hoarse protest, before it disappeared back under the surface.

Jeff lurched on board. His face was pink, squeezed tight by his protective hood and he peeled his head free, sat on the back of the boat.

'Glad to see you working hard, Miles,' he said.

Miles looked at the tin cup in his hands. He had only taken a few sips but he chucked the rest over the side and returned the cup to the cabin. He walked over to Jeff, picked up his flippers, gloves and hood and put them in the fresh water bucket. And he could hear Jeff's breathing, over the sound of the water and the sound of the engine. Jeff's heavy breath. And he stayed where he was for a long time. He didn't even try to get up. He just sat there, the skin on his face still pink.

Martin paced around the boat. He held the slack airline in his hands and looked out at the water. Miles watched his eyes, the way they skimmed back and forth over the surface. Dad had been down for a long time.

Miles looked over the side.

Below in the murky darkness, in the swirling kelp, all you had to guide you was one hand touching the rock wall while your legs kicked you down blind. And that's where they were, the abalone. Down where the algae grew thick, where the continental shelf dropped away. They could eat their way across kilometres of submerged rock, those creatures. And there were caves and crevices, places to get stuck. Places where the air hose could get snagged.

Miles had only been down once, but that was enough. He'd been scared of the darkness and of the kelp wrapping around his legs. He'd been scared of the heavy feeling in his chest. And it made his head buzz like crazy, the pressure. The weight of all that water.

In a few years he would have to dive down there for real.

Dad surfaced close to the rocks and Martin had him. He pulled him in. And Dad was still in the water when he ripped his mouthpiece away, let out a roar.

'Jesus,' he said. 'Jesus!'

He was still saying Jesus when he clambered on deck. He'd brought up two full bags and the abs were huge.

'A few days of this! A few days of this and we're back.'

He looked at Miles and he smiled.

*H*arry put his parka on and picked up the Redskins show bag he'd got for Stuart. He wasn't meant to walk around by himself, not if he wasn't going to Aunty Jean's, but he thought going to Stuart's would be OK. Anyway, Dad wouldn't know.

He walked through to the lounge and slipped his feet into his rubber gumboots. They were freezing. He thought about grabbing another pair of socks, but he couldn't be bothered. His feet would warm up if he walked fast.

He'd walk fast.

Outside, the light was flat and even, the same grey light that there always was. Sometimes right in the middle of the day the sun shone bright and broke through, but it never made anything warm. Not the air or the ground. Not really.

At the end of the drive Harry turned onto the gravel road. He listened for cars. Listened for trucks. He checked for dust clouds up ahead. It was clear.

After his house there weren't any houses for a while, not near the river, anyway. The place was thick with trees, black with them, and there wasn't anything else but trees until you crossed the bridge and went round the long corner. After that, where the road was straight, there was scrub and rectangles of cleared land full of weeds. A few old fire tracks. A few old farmhouses. Not much.

But that's where Stuart lived. He lived in a caravan. It was a caravan with a wooden shed attached so it was like a house, really. And Harry didn't think that it could even move anymore, the caravan, because it had been in one place for so long. It had been there for all of Stuart's life, maybe even longer, and it had sunk down into the earth so that its wheels were almost buried.

Stuart's mum's white Ford Cortina wasn't in the drive, but Harry walked up to the door and knocked anyway.

No one answered.

Maybe they had gone to set up the stall. Stuart's mum grew berries, raspberries and blackberries, and she sold them on the road just outside of Huonville.

She usually just left an honesty box but sometimes, on the weekends or holidays when there were people from Hobart driving down, she would stay at the stall. Stuart hated it when he had to stay there, but at least he got to go to Huonville and look at all the shops. It was better than hanging around here.

Harry put the show bag by the door. He rolled it up in case it rained, and then he walked away. But he didn't walk fast now. He took his time. Stuart and his mum might drive past. They might come back.

A truck appeared when he was nearly back at the bridge. Harry stood in the ditch and closed his eyes tight against the grit that kicked up in his face, against the wind. And he could smell the sap, even over all the dust. He could smell the freshly cut trees – the smell of crushed leaves.

When he opened his eyes, the truck was lost in a haze of smoke and gravel and dust. There wouldn't be another truck for a while.

He walked onto the bridge and leant against the railings on one side. The dark water of Lune River was moving with a silent speed that made the hairs on the back of his neck stand up. He picked up a rock and dropped it over the edge. It disappeared instantly into the rushing water and didn't even leave a mark on the surface.

You would need a million rocks to make a dent.

He looked for bigger rocks on the side of the road to chuck into the river, and he nearly stepped on a dead bandicoot. It was in perfect nick, its stripy fur and speckled white cheeks still intact. Harry bent down to inspect it closely. Only a dried trickle of blood coming from the corner of its mouth gave away that it was dead and not just asleep. And it must be pretty fresh, because it hadn't been eaten by quolls or devils or been picked up by a wedgetail yet.

Joe collected roadkill. Only the good ones, though. He stripped away all the fur and flesh, then rebuilt the skeletons – like the megafauna at the Hobart Museum, only smaller. The biggest one he had was a wallaby, but Harry liked the Tassie devil best, with its big jaw and sharp teeth. Harry wondered whether he should take the bandicoot around to Joe's place. It wouldn't take that long, maybe an hour.

Something moved in the grass ahead. The tail and then the small face of a dog. A pup. It had just come right out of the bushes and it sniffed over the dead bandicoot, looked up at Harry. Harry checked to see if anyone was with the dog, then he knelt down, let the dog lick his face. And he cuddled the dog. It was a kelpie. He could tell because of its smile – the red-brown mouth rimmed by tan, unable to hide its joy. Harry was glad, too.

The pup wagged its tail, started walking away from the road, and it looked back to see if Harry was going to follow. He did, and the dog led him into a thick pocket of trees. Harry picked up a stick, whistled, and threw it, and the pup grabbed the stick in its mouth and ran ahead. Harry ran, too. He chased the dog through the scrub, chased it all the way out into a clearing. And there was a long bogged-up paddock. There was an old wooden shack.

Suddenly Harry knew where he was.

This was George Fuller's place.

Kids at school were scared of George Fuller. Harry had only ever seen him once, standing on the side of the road, but he didn't ever want to see him again. His face was all squashed in and he looked like a monster. Stuart said that he lured people to his shack and ate them. Other kids said worse things. They said that George had killed his parents, burnt them alive, while they were sleeping in their beds, and that he was crazy. Harry never came this way. And if he had to, he was always careful to stick close to the road instead of taking the short cut.

The dog dropped the stick and trotted closer to the shack. It took a few gulps of water from a yellow bucket then ran straight back to Harry with an old bit of rope in its mouth. It dumped the rope at Harry's feet. Harry looked at the shack. He couldn't see any signs of George so, with one eye on the house, he picked up the fat knotted rope and chucked it as far as he could. The dog was fast. It took an aerial leap, had the rope in its mouth before it had time to reach the ground.

'Good boy,' Harry said quietly. 'Drop it. Drop the rope.'

He grabbed one side of the rope and tugged. He pulled as hard as he could, almost lifted the pup off the ground, but the dog held on, growled and pulled back.

There was a creak, a door opening, and Harry bolted. He ran as fast as he could, only looking back when he had nearly reached the safety of the trees. George Fuller was standing there by his shack, and he was waving.

Harry's leg hit something. Something sharp and he fell hard, smacked the ground. Hot pain shot up his shin and he grabbed at his leg. Someone called out his name.

He jumped up, kept running and he didn't look back or stop until he made it to the bridge. There he hung onto the rail, caught his breath. He checked his shin. The skin was grazed but it wasn't bleeding much.

There had been no one else around.

How could that man know his name?

*J*oe was waiting there for him when the boat came in. Waiting in the orange van. And when Dad said he could go, Miles ran.

Everything you needed was in that van: surfboards, sleeping bags, fishing gear, tools. Miles opened the door and could smell hot chips and gravy. There was a pile left for him on the middle seat, lukewarm and soggy but still good.

'I'm sorry you have to work,' Joe said.

Miles shrugged. He didn't want to talk about it.

Joe drove fast on the raw dusty gravel and plumes of it billowed up behind them. Scrub and shacks passed the window. Kit homes, most tiny, bare fibro, unpainted. Miles knew them all. Their gardens full of rusty car shells, dead tractors, decaying boats marooned on land. And if you didn't know better, you'd think that no one lived here anymore. That all these places were abandoned. But people were in there somewhere, hidden and burrowed in. They were there.

The road began to climb. Less shacks, more scrub, and on the other side was Roaring. Joe stopped the car right on the headland, parked close to the cliff, and Miles looked down at the bluff, down at the reefs. He turned to Joe and smiled.

There was swell coming in. It was clean. No wind.

They were going in.

Miles could get into his wetsuit so fast, even when it was damp and stuck to your skin like glue. You couldn't wait around when the surf was good. You couldn't wait around and say, I'll surf it later, because the wind changed and the tide changed and just like that, it could go onshore. Just like that, it could get fat with the high tide and you could miss it.

He grabbed his board and ran down the steep track to the beach. He left Joe behind. And all the way down his eyes were out on that break. The right-hander that wrapped tight around the bluff. It was his. He'd get there first, get the first wave.

The cold water bit at his hands and feet as he began the paddle. Winter brought massive swells, awesome to watch and not much fun to be in, but today the bluff was still like liquid mercury. Near perfect three-foot lines. The paddle was easy. The waves were easy. The ocean was at peace.

He sat behind the break, looked back towards the beach. Joe was only just coming down the track, but he was strong. He paddled quick and he'd be out in no time. Miles turned his head to the horizon and grinned. A good-sized line, maybe a four-footer, hit the reef and began to peel. Sometimes you didn't have to move an inch. The shoulder of the wave lifted his board; he looked down the clean face and took the drop. Miles felt his bones. He carved along the wave nice and loose, flicked up with sharp cutbacks every so often to bring him back up onto the shoulder. He heard Joe hooting from the beach and he knew he was charging.

Joe and Miles sat together waiting for one last line.

And then Joe said he was leaving.

Miles sat still. He looked down at the water. It was one solid dark mass, impossible to see past the surface now that the light had gone.

'The boat's done. Just gotta get a few things sorted. Pack up the house. Maybe you could come over and help on the weekend.'

Joe's boat was finished, the one he had been building all these years. It was ready to sail, ready to take Joe away.

'She's a fucking bitch,' Miles said. And it was true, Aunty Jean was a bitch. Granddad had left the house to Joe. He had lived with Granddad since he was thirteen. Aunty Jean stole it from him, contested the will.

'You know she's going to put money aside for you. For you and Harry. Anyway, it's not even about the house really. It's –'

'It's what?'

Joe splashed some water on his face. He didn't answer.

'It's what?'

'Time,' Joe said. 'It's just time.'

Everything was dark blue now. The cliffs and the beach and even Joe's face were all blurred and hazy. Miles wanted to tell Joe that things were bad at home. He wanted to tell him that working on the boat was bad and that he didn't know what to do. But he didn't say any of that. He just said he would come and help on the weekend. Come and pack up the shed and house. Because he wanted to stay at Granddad's. He wanted to stay with Joe.

'We'd better go in,' Joe said. 'It's freezing.'

Miles had started to shiver, but he couldn't really feel it.

*I*t was still dark outside, but light was coming in from under the door and Miles was coughing.

'Are you sick?' Harry asked.

'Shut your eyes for a sec. I've gotta turn the light on.'

Harry closed his eyes tight but the burst of bright light still made his eyes water. He opened them carefully, held one hand up to shield them. Miles coughed again from somewhere deep, and he had black bags under his eyes. They were puffy.

'Are you sick? Maybe you can stay home?'

If Miles stayed home they could put the fire on and watch TV, and Harry could make him cup-a-soups and lemon drinks. Miles squeezed a jumper over the top of the one he already had on and put his beanie on.

'Go back to sleep,' he said.

'Do you want my scarf?'

'I'm OK.'

The air was cold and Harry was glad he didn't have to get out of bed. He let his body lie back down. Dad called Miles from the lounge.

'Maybe you'll get to finish early today?' Harry said.

Miles was looking for something on the floor. He picked up some socks and slipped them on over the ones he was already wearing.

'I'd better go.' He coughed again and turned the bedroom light off.

Harry heard the toaster pop, then the front door shut. Miles had left the lounge light on for Harry so it wasn't dark. He curled up in his doona, but he knew he wouldn't be able to sleep now. He was already awake. He was thinking about that dog. The puppy that wanted to play with him. And he knew he was going to go back and look for it. He knew that's what he was going to do. Maybe not today, but soon.

*T*hey had finished up early.

All the tubs were full – their daily quota reached – and they would get back to the wharf by eleven, have the boat cleaned and ready by twelve, maybe. Miles was thinking that he'd walk around to Joe's from the wharf and see if he was home. Because when the boat had passed Tasman Head the swell had been running straight south-west and if it stayed that way, and if the sea breeze didn't kick up, there'd be good waves at low tide at Lady Bay or on the bluff at Roaring. It would be perfect.

Martin poked his head out of the cabin and the engine cut.

He'd seen salmon.

Miles ran to the side, looked out the back. Atlantic salmon were massing in a giant ball – a feeding frenzy – and they were huge, probably escapees from the salmon cages in Dover. An easy catch.

Dad grabbed a rod and cast out. The metal lure only floated for a second before he yanked it back and a salmon hit the deck with a thud, gills flaring. Miles ran over and grabbed it. The fish fought hard against his hands but he managed to unhook its jaw and chuck it in a plastic tub. As soon as the line was free, Dad cast again and just as quickly, there was another fish. Jeff grabbed a rod, too, and now fish were flying in every few seconds. Miles scrambled around on the deck, unhooking fish and sliding them into the tub. Within minutes the first tub was full. Miles knelt down and watched the fat salmon writhing, their sharp little teeth trying to find something to bite. Atlantic salmon were vicious little bastards.

Martin came over and with a swift stab to the bottom of the head, he killed the fish one by one. It wasn't cruel if you did it properly, but Miles wasn't very good at it. He always hesitated at the last minute and he was glad he didn't have to do it today.

Martin put his knife down.

Something made them both look up.

A change in light – a sudden stillness.

There was a giant mako in the sky, its mouth closing in on the salmon at the end of Dad's line.

Miles tried to stand, tried to move, but Jeff pushed past him and he fell face first onto the wet deck. The whole boat quaked, tipped and Miles slid until he smashed hard against the railings. And water was coming in; coming in or coming over, and when he looked the ocean was right there, right next to his face. He was pinned, the side of his body numb. He turned his head slowly and the thick, steel blue skin of the shark was touching his arm, touching his skin. It was squeezing into him, thrashing wildly. The shark was right on him.

He felt something grab his legs. It was Martin, pulling hard – so hard it hurt. Miles's ribs felt like they were going to cave in, let everything give way, and there was a sickening crack. Miles waited for the pain. He waited for the air to be sucked out of his chest, but someone else was yelling. Someone else was broken.

The shark's tail had hit Martin's legs and he was down. Down on top of Miles.

Now Miles could hardly even move his head. All he could do was watch the shark beside him fight. It was jerking itself back, inch by inch, in the direction it had come. Miles could see the curved teeth that spilled out in every direction, teeth that brushed against his skin. And the shark's eye was on him now,

53

full of strength and pride. The eye of a champion – a wolf of the sea.

'We're going over!'

Dad was yelling from the far side of the deck. The boat must have been up on some crazy angle because he seemed to be hanging from the rails.

They were going over, tipping over.

They were going to go in the water.

A crack ripped through the air, an explosion that blew his ears apart. The shark began thrashing harder, stronger, and Miles could hardly breathe.

'No!' Martin shouted. He was trying to drag his body up and cover Miles. 'Don't shoo –'

Another crack and someone was laughing. Jeff was laughing.

Miles could see a bullet wound, blood oozing from the mako's head. It shook and jumped, every movement bringing the water closer, and Jeff was closer now, standing right above Miles on a weird angle. He was still laughing when the shark's teeth gnashed across his shins, ripping his skin open. Jeff made a hissing sound, cocked his rifle and fired again.

Miles shut his eyes, sure that this bullet would lodge in his head, sure that he was dead now.

And he didn't move.

But he felt the boat move, right itself. He felt all the weight that was crushing him lift away. Someone dragged him to his feet. Dad. He was saying something. It looked like 'You OK?' or 'You're OK', but Miles couldn't hear the words. His ears were gone, stuffed full of ringing.

He stood there and watched Dad scramble to rescue debris that had been flung off the boat. The abs and salmon were gone, the tools and equipment. Almost the whole deck was cleared except for the ten-foot mako that now took up the whole mid-section of the boat. Miles looked down at his arms, his body. That shark hadn't hurt him – not even a scratch.

She lay on her side, her blue skin already turning grey, and Miles felt sick as he watched Jeff slice through her white underbelly with ease. Her stomach and insides slid through blood onto the deck.

She was pregnant.

Jeff hacked into the full womb and three pups spilled out; two dead and half eaten, the other trying to swim in its mother's blood against the hard surface of the deck, tiny gills stretched open, black eyes searching. Jeff bent over and stabbed it through the head, grinning as its body came up on the long knife, still fighting. He chucked it at Miles and laughed as he wiped blood off his face.

Miles caught the baby in his arms. It was dead now, black eyes fixed.

It was fully formed, more than half a metre long, maybe only days away from being born. It would have survived if Jeff had just let it go, let it slide off the back of the boat. It had made it this far, battling its siblings, killing and feeding off them. Waiting. It would have been born strong, ready to hunt, ready to fight.

Miles felt the engine through his boots. They were moving, but Jeff was still busy with his prize, busy decapitating her. He hooked the head on the winch and started pulling it up. The grotesque and bloodied thing rose, bullet wounds clearly visible; all three to the head, the last right between the eyes. With a metal rod, Jeff slid the rest of the hacked-up carcass down and off the back of the boat, leaving a trail of blood and flesh in the water for the birds to pick through.

Someone whacked into Miles from behind. He turned and Dad was yelling, red in the face, pointing at Martin who was slumped against the wall of the cabin. Miles was still holding the dead baby shark in his hands and Dad grabbed it and chucked it over the side. Then he slapped Miles hard in the face.

'I can't hear,' Miles managed to say, or yell, but Dad just marched him into the cabin and made him take the wheel.

Martin looked bad. The sweat on his face, the colour of his skin. The shark had snapped his leg so easily. It was swollen and strangely twisted so that it barely looked attached from the knee down. Miles thought that some of Martin's ribs might be broken, too, because of the way he was breathing shallow and quick. But that could have just been because of the pain. It would take at least twenty minutes to get to Dover and then another thirty to the hospital at Huonville. Miles prayed that the painkillers would start working soon, and that his hearing would come back.

He jumped up on the tray of the ute and sat next to Martin who was propped up in the corner. Dad had carefully put blankets all around him and patted him on the shoulder before getting in the cab. It seemed to Miles that Dad genuinely cared for Martin. There was something between them, something that went back a long way.

The ute choked into life. Miles's hearing was coming back in waves. He watched Jeff walk across the road to the pub and was glad he wasn't coming to the hospital. Martin was still sweating, still pale.

'Not long now,' Miles said, still unsure of the volume of his voice.

Martin attempted a small smile and gestured for Miles to come closer. Miles was careful not to touch Martin's leg as he moved.

'Your dad's gonna need you,' he said.

And suddenly Miles knew what that busted leg meant. He wouldn't be going to school next term. He'd be out on that boat with Dad and with Jeff until Martin could come back. He'd be stuck out there every day.

'Watch Jeff. I've tried telling your dad, but . . .'

Martin broke off. He rested his head against the cab of the ute.

Miles sat back, too, and watched the white lines of the road snake out from under the tray. He watched it all get further and further away – the fishing boats and Dover, the smoke from the cannery. He watched until they were gone from sight and there was nothing but the road and the green grass and the marshy Huon River flowing slowly.

An elderly nurse ushered Miles down the corridor into a small office as the orderlies moved Martin from the ute. She pushed him down onto a low office chair in front of an electric bar heater and said she'd be back in a minute. Miles watched her waddle off down the corridor and disappear.

Huonville Hospital was small, made out of the same yellow brick and big steel-framed windows as Dover High, except the hospital was only one storey; a flat rectangle with a car park. Miles had been here when it was brand new, when it smelled of paint and lino. And he'd thought it was lucky there was a hospital so close when Granddad was sick. It meant it was easy to come and visit.

But it hadn't been easy. He'd only gone once.

Granddad was on his side, all bony and yellow with tubes in his arms and a mask covering most of his face. He was crumpled like a sheet of old newspaper and the room was full of gurgling, each breath slow and full of fluid. Granddad was drowning on the inside, and Miles just stood at the door like a coward.

He should have walked over, should have held his hand. But he didn't. He ran down the corridor and

59

out to the car park and he told Dad that Granddad was asleep and that the nurse had told him to come back tomorrow.

When they got home, Joe phoned to say that Granddad had died.

'It's all right. Your friend's going to be fine – just a broken leg.'

The nurse had an arm around his shoulder and Miles realised that his gumboots were red hot from the electric heater. He wiped his cheeks.

'It's probably just the shock. Here, I brought you some tea.'

But Miles didn't have time to drink it because Dad came and found him and said they were going.

*H*arry found the bushes where he had first seen the dog and he stood there hidden from the road. He called out 'Here boy' quietly and waited, but the dog didn't come. If only he knew the dog's name then maybe it would come back and they could play here by the road. Harry could even take the dog home for a while and give it some milk or something to eat. Dad wouldn't know.

He called out again, louder this time, and looked into the scrub. You couldn't see George's house or even his front paddock from here. You could only see trees. Maybe he'd be safe if he stayed behind the line of trees. If he saw George he could run. George was big and all hunched over so he probably wouldn't be able to run fast. Not like Harry could.

He'd just walk a little way, just to see if he could find the dog.

There was a track, a kind of path that he hadn't noticed before. It was muddy and slippery with leaves and Harry was glad he had worn his gumboots and not his sneakers. There were probably leeches here. He walked slowly and he kept on listening.

He looked up: some of the eucalypts were really tall – straight and tall and full at the top, blocking out the sky. He heard sticks and branches crack, but he knew that sound. It was always there if you listened, always there in the distance, even when there was no wind. It was the sound of the crack wattle cracking. The sound of the wattle dropping branches into the river. And upstream, on tight bends and narrow channels, there were so many branches that they almost dammed the water. They almost choked it. But downstream the current was strong. The water just swallowed the sticks and branches and flushed them out to sea.

Harry turned a corner and suddenly he could see it, the paddock and the shack.

He'd reached the end of the trees.

He crouched down. He couldn't see George, but the dog was there. It was lying flat on the verandah in a small patch of sunlight that had broken through the clouds. It looked like it was fast asleep.

Harry stayed still and watched the dog. He wanted to sit down because his legs were hurting and it felt like maybe they were going to sleep, but when he touched the ground with his hands it was wet here, too. He'd just have to stay crouching.

The dog really was asleep. It hadn't moved at all, not even its tail or ears. Maybe Harry should go and come back in a while. Come back later.

But then the dog raised its head. There was the creak of a spring and the door of the shack opened. Harry held his breath, stayed perfectly still as George stepped out onto the verandah. His bent legs were burning but he didn't flinch. He didn't move.

George had something in his hand. A toolbox, and he put it down on the verandah. Then he turned and went back inside. It was Harry's chance to get away.

He stood up, held onto a tree to steady himself. He was sure he hadn't made a sound, but when he looked the dog was standing, its ears up, face pointed right at Harry. And then it barked.

Harry pushed his body flat against the tree. He wanted to run but his legs were asleep. They were just dead weights hanging and they wouldn't work, wouldn't move. He pushed his face into the bark.

He closed his eyes and tried to be invisible. Maybe the dog hadn't seen him. Maybe it was barking at a bird or a rabbit or a snake. But there was another bark and it was close. Harry looked up and he saw the dog running. He swung around and the dog was already at his feet, jumping and whining and clawing at his legs. Harry searched wildly, but George hadn't followed. He was standing outside the shack.

Harry could feel the blood moving in his legs again. They were coming back to life and he could sprint away now, but he just kept looking at the wooden shack and then back at the dog. And the dog's blue eyes were gleaming and its tail was wagging and it started to pull at the sleeve of his jacket.

Harry let the dog pull. He let the dog pull him away from the safety of the trees. And he moved, step by step down the muddy paddock. He moved step by step, closer to the shack, because there was nowhere else to go and nothing to do and because the dog wanted him to stay.

When he got down to the verandah near George, the dog became still. It sat down. Harry rubbed its head, scratched behind its ears. He tried not to look at George's face.

'I like your dog,' he said quietly.

George seemed to have trouble speaking, the way his mouth was all open and had a big hole at the top, but Harry could hear the words. He could hear that the dog's name was Jake and that he was six months old.

'I'm Harry,' he said, and George nodded. It looked like maybe he was smiling.

George walked to the door and he waved for Harry to follow before he went inside. The wooden door sprang closed behind him.

There was smoke coming from the chimney and it was probably really warm inside. Harry had forgotten his gloves and his ears were cold. He dug his hands into Jake's brown fur but the dog kept moving. It just wanted to play.

Harry stood up. He stepped onto the small verandah, stood in front of the door. He wished he could see inside without having to open the door. There could be anything in there. Anything waiting for him. It could be a trap and no one would know he was here. He took a deep breath and reached out for the door handle. The door creaked open.

Harry looked into the darkened room. George was standing by a table pouring hot water into a teapot. Jake pushed between Harry's legs and went inside. Harry felt warm air on his face and he followed.

George pulled out a chair and Harry sat down. He looked at the table, watched George's big strange hands put milk and two sugars in each cup before he poured the tea. It was exactly how Harry had his tea, milk and two sugars. He looked up into George's face, but he wasn't looking at Harry. He was looking down at the cups as he stirred the tea with a spoon. He slid a cup over to Harry.

'Thanks,' Harry said, and he took the cup in his hands.

George sat down.

From the outside, this place looked just like a picker's hut, all weathered up and grey. But the inside was bright and neat and clean and Harry thought it was nicer than where he lived, nicer than the brown house, even though it was just one room and there was only a sink instead of a bathroom and the toilet must be outside somewhere down the back. There were even fresh flowers in a vase. White flowers. Lilies.

Harry drank his tea quickly because he didn't know what else to do. He didn't know what to say and he was glad when Jake came over and put his head on Harry's lap. He patted Jake's head and then he just started talking. He told George that he really loved dogs and that he wished he could have one at

home but Dad wouldn't let him because he hated
dogs. He told George that Miles wanted a dog, too,
and that he wished Miles didn't have to work out on
the boat because he didn't like being on his own all
school holidays, and he couldn't go to Joe's because
Joe was busy because he had to pack up Granddad's
house and everything. And then he asked George if
he had known Granddad and George nodded. And
Harry thought he would have because back then
everyone knew everyone around here. That's what
Granddad had told him anyway.

George didn't say much, but he seemed to be
listening. He seemed to understand what Harry was
talking about. Harry asked him where he got Jake
and he waited for George to answer. George poured
them both another cup of tea, stirred the milk and
sugar in like before, and then he took a sip.

He said that he found Jake on the road near Daryl
Jarratt's place, and that he was skinny and sick and
that he was almost dead.

Harry knew exactly how Daryl Jarratt's dogs
lived. They were wild, spent their lives on the end
of a chain frothing at the mouth and whining and
barking and looking like they might want to kill
something. Looking like they might want to die.
He'd seen them once from behind the windshield

of Dad's ute – eyes red and full, spit dripping from their barking mouths as Daryl chucked a bucket of rotten scraps on the ground.

Dad had gone up there to buy a chainsaw. He'd said that Daryl was desperate, selling everything, even his car and it was all as cheap as you liked. And Dad had laughed about the chainsaw when they got home because he didn't even need one. He already owned a better one. He said he would sell Daryl's chainsaw for twice what he paid for it.

'Bloody fool,' he'd said.

Harry never went anywhere near that place again. Even though they were almost neighbours. He never went anywhere near that red metal sign on a chain that hung over the bottom of the driveway, big letters painted in white. *Private Property.*

Harry looked down at Jake. He was lying on the floor now and Harry stroked down his body, patted his warm stomach. The dog's eyes fell heavy and then they closed. And he was asleep just like that. Asleep with his head resting on Harry's foot.

Jake was lucky. George had saved him.

George put his cup down on the table and stretched his arms out by his sides. Harry didn't know what time it was. He didn't know how long he had been sitting there. His foot had started to go to sleep again under Jake's head and he lifted his leg gently off the ground. Jake woke, got to his feet. Then he curved his back into a big stretch, yawned. He looked at Harry.

'I'd better go,' Harry said.

George stood up and they walked out onto the verandah. The cold air hit Harry's face hard and he zipped up his parka. George picked up the toolbox that was still on the verandah. He said he had to make some repairs to his jetty down the back. He said Harry could come if he wanted.

'I'd better go,' Harry said again, even though he didn't really have to. He stepped off the verandah.

But then he stopped. He turned back to George.

'I might come back again, though,' he said. 'Another day.'

George nodded and Harry watched him walk away with Jake following close behind.

*M*iles began hosing down the deck and ice-cold spray showered his face and hands. If it wasn't for the ache in his ribs and the bullet hole in the deck, he might have thought that yesterday had never happened, because everything was normal. They'd just gone out like normal. Only Martin was gone. Only that was different.

Jeff left early as usual and Dad was in the cabin. Miles walked in as he turned the engine over. It didn't sound good. It spluttered and shook, had sounded like that all day. And they had hardly found anything at the Friars. The huge abs that had been there yesterday were gone. There was nothing at Tasman Head, either. Nothing anywhere, no matter how many times Dad went down.

'Will we be able to go out tomorrow?' Miles asked.

Dad didn't answer. Miles should have backed away. He should have left Dad alone, but he didn't. He wanted the engine to be broken.

'It sounds bad. The engine sounds –'

Dad slammed his hands down on the dash.

'You think I can just pick and choose when we go out? You think I have a fucking choice?' He turned to Miles, clenched his fists.

'Get out of here,' he said.

Miles backed out of the cabin, but Dad suddenly pushed past him and jumped off the boat. Miles watched him march down the wharf. He stopped at the ute for a minute and Miles thought that he might get in and just drive off, but he didn't. He kept walking. He walked across the road. He was going to the pub.

Miles stood on the deck. He wasn't sure what to do. The boat couldn't stay here. This spot on the wharf would be needed in the morning for the cray boats and the night trawlers. Miles looked over to their mooring site in the middle of the bay. It was marked by a pink buoy and the dinghy was there waiting. One of Mr Roberts's big 40-foot dive boats, *Reef Runner II*, was pulling in nearby. He had three of them, now, all white fibreglass, clean and new. They dwarfed Dad's boat, made her seem more wrecked than she was, more faded.

Miles would have to move the boat himself.

He tugged on the thick rope that kept the boat secured to the wharf, but the loop of rope wouldn't budge from the stumpy pole. He climbed up onto the wharf, stood as close as possible to the edge and wrenched the loop free. He threw the thick rope on deck, leapt after it, and bolted to the cabin. By the time he got the engine into drive the boat had pulled out metres from the wharf.

But getting to the moorings was the easy part.

The dinghy was always hard to start, especially in winter. Miles pushed the prime button three times to give himself the best chance. He pulled the cord as hard as he could and it nearly caught. Nearly. He tried again but it wasn't close this time. He tried five more times. Nothing. Dad usually got it on the second or third go, but after twelve attempts, Miles was panting. And he was coughing again. Sweating.

He primed the engine again, pushing the soft button that squirted diesel around inside, and he pulled with all he had, with his whole body. He *had* to get it started. *Had* to get it this time. But it didn't start. He let go of the cord and coughed into his hands. He sat down. He'd have to rest for a bit then try again.

Another dinghy started. Miles looked up and saw Mr Roberts putting in his direction. He waved and Miles waved back.

'Jump in. We'll tow it.'

Mr Roberts held the dinghies together while Miles hopped over. He hadn't thought about what he'd do if he couldn't start the dinghy. There wasn't much he could do.

'Finishing up on your own today, Miles?' he said.

'Nah – I mean, I asked if I could do it by myself.'

Miles looked away. He was embarrassed at the lie. Mr Roberts had probably seen Dad storm off, and he knew Dad, what he was like.

Back at the wharf Miles said goodbye, but he didn't have anywhere to go. He walked up to the ute. It was locked. He couldn't even wait in the car. And he didn't want to go into the pub. Not until he was totally desperate, anyway. Aunty Jean's house wasn't too far away, but he didn't want to go there. He didn't want to ask her for anything. He could walk to Joe's and see if he was home. It was only a forty-minute walk, but if he wasn't there he was stuck.

'I'll give you a lift.'

It was Mr Roberts again. He was suddenly right there behind him.

'It's out of your way,' Miles said, and he covered his mouth as he started to cough again. Mr Roberts pulled something out of his pocket. It was a packet of Butter Menthols.

'I'll just go and tell your dad then,' he said.

Miles watched Mr Roberts cross the road and go into the pub. He was a tall man. He was like a bear and Dad didn't like him much. No one did since he'd got rich off abalone, since he'd bought three new boats and built a new house and sent his kids to private school. But it was strange. Mr Roberts didn't seem to care about what other people thought. He really didn't. It was the way he walked, the way he talked and laughed like he wasn't scared of anything. And maybe he really wasn't scared of anything.

People said he'd been lucky, but Miles thought he'd been smart. He'd built up slowly so that no one even noticed. And he didn't sell to the cannery like everyone else. He took his catch up to Hobart where the larger abs got more money, and were snap-frozen and sent to Asia whole, shells and all.

He'd started like all of them. He'd started back when Dad and Nick had.

Miles got in the passenger seat of Mr Roberts's station wagon and sucked on a Butter Menthol. It was the newest, nicest car he'd ever been in. The seats were covered in thick, soft material and the heater blew warm air as soon as they started moving.

'Mr Roberts? I'm still a bit wet. Should I sit on a towel or something?'

Mr Roberts shook his head. He slapped his leg to show Miles that his pants were wet, too. 'I'm always a bit damp,' he said. 'Anyway, call me Brian. Nobody calls me Mr Roberts except for Justin's new headmistress. I forget her name. Cleary or something. Real piece of work.'

Mr Roberts laughed and Miles smiled too. It was hard to imagine Justin Roberts at a private school in a uniform and wearing a tie with that long floppy hair of his that hung down over his eyes so that you could only see his big mouth and his teeth sticking out.

'Is he doing all right?' Miles asked.

'Only thing he likes is the footy team. Good apparently. Haven't been up to see a game, but he'll be down here next week. You boys should catch up for a wave.'

Miles nodded even though he knew Justin and he probably wouldn't see each other. He hadn't seen him for ages, not out in the water, anyway. They used to be friends, used to surf, but that all felt like a long time ago now. A lifetime.

Mr Roberts drove slowly, even on the straight bit of road. He kept a steady pace and his knees hugged the bottom of the steering wheel, his hands resting loose on top. The windows were tinted, just slightly, so that the grey sky seemed to be a midnight blue. Miles would have liked to keep on driving for a long time. To rest down against the warm seat and listen to Mr Roberts talk. To keep on going until there was no more road.

But then he saw them, on the tight bend before the river.

Flowers tied to the tree. White lilies right there, tied to that river gum. Miles choked on his Butter Menthol. He grabbed madly at the door, felt the car pull over, and when he got the door open, he leant over and coughed out a pool of phlegm and spit and whatever was left of the Butter Menthol.

'Jesus! Are you all right?'

Mr Roberts was out of the car. He'd come round and was standing on the side of the road. Miles couldn't speak. He wiped his mouth, sat back in his seat. He didn't want to look at Mr Roberts, and he tried not to look outside at all, but his eyes kept finding that tree, kept staring at the tree and at the lilies until he knew that they were real. That the flowers were really there.

Like they had been after she died. For months and months. Fresh lilies on the tree.

Mr Roberts took his time getting back in the car and when he did he didn't start the engine.

'Butter Menthol went down the wrong way,' Miles said.

Mr Roberts didn't say anything. Not for a bit. He handed Miles a hankie.

'I never pass here without thinking of her, you know. Not without thinking of your mum. It must have been bloody terrible.'

Miles blew his nose on the hankie. He shut his eyes.

'I don't really remember,' he said.

When he opened his eyes, Miles looked at the tree again. It still had a scar, a line where the bark had never grown back. And it was amazing that it had survived at all. They had hit it so hard.

When they pulled up the drive Miles opened the passenger door. He went to get out but Mr Roberts put his hand on his shoulder, held him back.

'Don't you get stuck here with your dad,' he said. 'Don't you let him . . . You're too young to be out there working, Miles. It's not right.'

Miles felt the words sink right down inside him.

'You've had it rough enough,' he said.

And he let Miles go.

*T*he Milo had to last for ages. A month. But Miles looked bad. He looked tired, still coughing all the time and even though milk wasn't good for a cold, that's what Aunty Jean said anyway, there wasn't anything else. Harry wanted to make Miles the best hot Milo ever and it was still early and they could watch the afternoon cartoons and put the fire on.

He heaped four tablespoons of Milo into Miles's cup and the hot milk went dark brown. He sprinkled more Milo on the top, just a bit, and it looked good. It smelled good. But when he took the cup over, Miles's eyes were closed. He was already asleep, his head leaning back, resting on the top of the couch.

Harry sat down beside him holding the Milo.

'Miles?' he said quietly. 'Miles?'

But he didn't wake up.

Aunty Jean's house was white on the outside and white on the inside, and they had to leave their boots at the door. Sometimes she made them take off their socks as well in case they were damp and left marks on the thick new carpet. She always offered them clean socks to put on but Miles would never touch them. Anyway, the carpet felt nice on his bare feet, springy and soft, but the Saturday afternoon roast always took forever to cook.

It was some kind of dark meat this time. Beef, maybe, and it did taste good. The gravy was salty and it soaked into the roast potatoes. Miles ate fast. If they got out of Aunty Jean's soon, there would be time for a surf with Joe when he picked them up. But when he finished he saw that Harry had barely touched his. He didn't like meat much. He'd only eaten the potatoes. It was driving Miles mad watching him move bits of meat and carrot around and around making rings of gravy on the plate.

'Try and eat some meat, Harry,' Aunty Jean said.

Harry looked at Miles and Miles stared back. He kicked Harry's leg under the table, but that didn't work. He wouldn't eat any more.

Aunty Jean put her knife and fork down on her plate and finally they were allowed to get up and take the dishes into the kitchen.

The clock above the cooker said it was 1:55 pm.

Miles filled the sink and started to wash the dishes. He squeezed the detergent hard, made the water slimy and full of suds. And he washed like mad, lining the dishes up neatly in the rack until it was full.

Aunty Jean came into the kitchen and put the kettle on. She got out three teacups and put them on the bench.

'I don't want any tea,' Miles said, and he picked up the tea towel, began drying the plates.

Aunty Jean crumpled up her nose. 'Well, I do,' she said.

'I'll have one,' Harry called from the dining room.

Miles knew he just wanted the biscuits that came with the tea.

'I'll cut your hair after,' Jean said. 'You both need it.'
And then she smiled.

They were stuck.

Miles watched Harry squirm on the stool in the
kitchen as Aunty Jean pulled at his hair with the
comb.

Every time he tried to move his head, she grabbed
his face and held him still.

'That's what you get for having curly hair, young
man,' she said.

She wasn't even a bit like Mum. It was hard to
believe they were sisters because Aunty Jean was like
an old lady.

She dressed like an old lady and she smelled like
an old lady and she had arthritis like an old lady.

And he hoped they hurt, her fat knees. Her puffy
ankles that spilled over her shoes. All that fluid
moving around when she walked. Moving around
but never going away.

'Go to the cupboard and get a towel,' she said
suddenly, and when Miles looked up she was staring
right at him.

He turned away, walked down the hall. The linen
cupboard was huge and there were piles of sheets and
pillowcases and quilts and Miles didn't know what

the hell they were all for. Aunty Jean lived alone. She had been alone for ages, since Uncle Nick, and no one ever came to visit except them and they never stayed over. Never.

The towels were on a shelf at eye height and they were all white. There were no other colours, not even cream. It was weird. Miles pulled one out but they were packed in so tight that about five came loose and fell on the floor. He bent down to pick them up and there was a wooden box at the bottom of the cupboard. It was a big box, pushed right to the back – old wood, dark like blackwood. He had never seen it before.

He looked down the hall. He could hear Aunty Jean talking, but the door to the kitchen was closed just enough so that he couldn't see her.

He squatted down, pulled the box out. It had brass handles and carved flowers on the lid.

Inside there were carefully folded things.

Soft things.

They were all baby things.

'Miles! The towel!'

Miles shut the lid and slid the box away. He picked up one of the towels and shoved the rest back in the cupboard without folding them.

While Aunty Jean cut his hair, he stared straight ahead. She talked on and on about selling Granddad's house, but he just kept thinking about the box. He just kept thinking about the little blankets and the baby clothes and how all that stuff was perfect and clean and never used.

'What am I meant to do? What am I meant to do?' she kept saying.

And he heard her voice rise up, the familiar tears come.

'I grew up in that house, Miles. Don't I deserve something?'

Harry was sitting on the edge of the bath when Miles walked into the bathroom.

'Jesus,' he said, his curls all gone, his eyes bigger than normal because his hair was so short. And it made Miles smile, the way Harry just said Jesus like that, the way they both looked terrible like freshly shorn sheep.

Mum never used to cut Harry's hair short. She told him that curls were lucky and should be left alone. Harry liked that and he believed her. He believed everything. He even let her brush his hair every night without complaining.

Dad even brushed Harry's hair back then to stop it getting knotted.

Miles wiped his neck and face with the face washer to get the hair off before it started itching. His hair was really short. She may as well have just used the clippers.

'That's the last time,' Miles said.

Harry nodded but he didn't look convinced.

*B*y lunchtime the shed was half empty.

Out on the grass the 'throw away' pile was much smaller than the 'keep' pile thanks to Miles. He fought Joe over every piece of furniture and every tool, saying it was wrong to throw any of Granddad's stuff away. Harry agreed but he didn't say anything. He just tried to stay out of the way. He waited on the lawn until someone told him what to move and what he could touch and where to put things because he kept doing everything wrong. Most of the things in the shed were too heavy for him to lift and it was dark and full of cobwebs and he knew there were spiders in there. He'd already got two splinters from moving wood because there were no gloves that fit his hands. They were all too big. He should have just gone to Stuart's.

Joe took the first load of junk to the tip and Harry thought about going into the house and sitting down inside for a bit. It was cold and the wind was coming off the bay and Miles hadn't called or come out of the shed for ages. Maybe he'd gone in the house and Harry hadn't noticed.

Harry walked over and poked his head through the shed door. It seemed so much bigger inside now that it was half empty – big and dark. He couldn't see Miles anywhere.

'Miles?'

No answer. Harry stayed in the doorway anyway. There was still so much stuff in the shed. It was going to take them all day. They wouldn't be doing anything else. Just this.

'Miles?'

'I'm here,' he said. His voice came from down the back, behind a stack of old chairs. Harry made his way over, ducking through the spaces left between furniture. Miles was sitting down on a low seat leaning against the back wall of the shed.

'It's Mum's,' he said.

Harry didn't know what he was talking about. He looked on the ground and then behind him.

'It's from the car. The back seat from Mum's car.'

Harry looked at what Miles was sitting on. He couldn't tell what colour the seat was because there wasn't enough light, but he remembered that the seats in Mum's car were red, dark cherry red, and that they were always slippery and shiny and cold in the mornings. He remembered that the doors in the back had wooden panels that he could run his Matchbox cars along.

'You wouldn't remember,' Miles said.

Harry sat down next to Miles. 'I remember,' he said.

He ran his fingers along the cold leather. The seatbelts were still attached. He found the middle metal buckle, pressed the button with his finger. It still worked.

He looked at Miles. He didn't know why the seat was here. He didn't understand. Miles was staring ahead. Harry watched him slip both of his hands into the wide gap where the seat bottom and back joined. Harry remembered that his Matchbox cars used to end up there sometimes and Miles would fish them out for him.

He put one hand into the gap, too, but his fingers only found dust and grit. Then his hand touched the sticky threads of a spider web and he pulled it out quickly. He stood up.

Miles had something in his hand. He'd found something in the seat. Something small attached to a string.

'What is it?' Harry asked.

Miles held the string out for Harry to see. For him to take. And it was heavy. A big triangle of bone, sharp on the sides.

'What is it?'

'White pointer's tooth,' Miles said.

And he said it like he knew it. Like he was sure.

'Hello?'

It was Joe. Harry hadn't heard his van pull up, but he was standing in the light by the shed door.

Miles grabbed the tooth out of Harry's hand. He stood up and put it in his pocket.

'What are you doing back here?'

Joe bent over and picked up something from the ground. It was a steering wheel. He held it up in both hands.

'Jesus,' he said.

And Miles showed him the rest. The crumpled bumper bar, and bent doors. The whole boot and back axle. But he didn't show him the tooth.

Joe put the steering wheel down and wiped his hands on the front of his jeans.

'Maybe we should stop for a bit, have lunch.'

Outside, the light hurt Harry's eyes. Miles and Joe walked towards the house but Harry stayed on the grass. He shielded his eyes with his hand.

'What are we going to do with it?' he asked.

He knew Miles would never let Joe chuck Mum's seat out, take it to the tip. The seat and the steering wheel and whatever else was there would go on the 'keep' pile. They would keep it.

But Miles kept on walking. He went into the house. Joe stopped on the verandah, rested his arm on the railing.

'I don't know why Granddad kept all that stuff, but I don't think he should have. I don't think he should have kept those things.'

And he turned to go inside. He told Harry he'd make him a sandwich.

But Harry stayed where he was. He stayed among the piles of Granddad's things left on the lawn – all the things that were no longer needed, no longer useful – and he wished that Joe would stay.

*H*arry climbed into the passenger seat and closed the door. He liked going to the tip. Lots of devils had dens up there and they were slow and fat and almost tame from eating scraps and rotten food. Sometimes you could see them hanging around in the day, not like the ones near home that you could only hear late at night, growling and screaming and fighting when everything was dark. Sometimes Harry looked out the window and tried to see them. And sometimes he thought he saw eyes – little red eyes staring out through the scrub – but he was never sure. He knew Dad hated them, the sound they made. He knew if any devils ever made a den under the house then Dad would shoot them.

Harry hoped he would see some today.

They had found even more of the car as they emptied the shed, mostly dented panels, bits of the engine, and it was all loaded up in the trailer. The back of the van was full, too. There was so much junk at Granddad's that they would probably have to make four trips or more to the tip.

Joe backed out the drive and Harry waved to Miles. He was sitting on the verandah and he didn't wave back. He was meant to be going through the stuff in the house now, but Harry knew he would just sit there until they got back. He wanted to keep the house more than any of them. Joe didn't seem to mind much and Aunty Jean said it had to happen. 'We could all do with the money,' she said.

Harry just thought Granddad would be sad about all his stuff going to the tip.

Joe asked him if he was all right. 'Is it because I'm leaving?' he asked.

Harry shrugged. He wanted to wind down the window so he could breathe some cool air, but the car was kicking up so much dust off the road that he'd better not.

'I'm coming back, anyway. After I've seen a few places.'

'What places?' Harry asked.

'First stop, Samoa. From there who knows?'

'Where's Samoa?'

'South Pacific. You know, warm water, palm trees, white sand.'

Harry could picture places like that. He'd seen that stuff on TV, and suddenly he wanted to tell Joe about George Fuller. He wanted to tell Joe how he'd gone to George's place and had tea and played with his dog, Jake. He wanted to ask Joe if he knew George. George knew Granddad.

'Maybe Granddad kept the car because he thought he might find something?' he said, and he felt the van slow down, pull over.

Joe looked at him.

'What do you mean, Harry?'

Harry looked down at his legs. He wasn't sure.

'Maybe there was a man there, in the car,' he said. He wanted to say more about the man but he couldn't really remember.

'Do you mean the man from the ambulance?'

Harry shrugged. He didn't want to talk about it anymore. He couldn't remember why he'd said that now.

'You hit your head really hard. Remember? You had to go to hospital.'

Harry nodded. He remembered. Miles was in the ambulance, too, and his head was all cut up and bleeding and Harry had a grey blanket wrapped around him and someone kept saying 'You have to try and stay awake' over and over and they kept shaking him and he just wanted them to stop. He just wanted to go to sleep.

'When are you leaving?' Harry asked.

'Soon, mate. Soon.'

*M*iles walked down the path to the beach and sat down on the grey sand of Lady Bay. It was cloudy and overcast, but light was still reflecting off the water and it hurt his eyes. He squinted, let his eyes get used to the whiteness and he looked over all the familiar rocks and sand and water. He was meant to be going through the house but the house was full and stuffy and he didn't want to be in there.

He put his hand in his pocket, pulled out the string. He held it up to the light.

A shark's tooth, cold and sharp – a perfect blade.

Everything that a shark was rotted and disappeared; everything but its jaw and its teeth. That was all a shark could ever leave behind. And it was old, the tooth. It was yellow and old and he tried to picture it around Granddad's neck, or hanging up somewhere in the shed or in the workshop. And he tried to picture it in Mum's car, maybe swaying from the rear-view mirror, or sitting loose on the dash. He couldn't place it. He didn't know it.

'What's that?'

Miles looked up. It was Gary Bones standing there. Gary Bones. The big full forward who took hard marks and broke grown men. He grabbed the string out of Miles's hand, tucked the tooth up tight inside his fist.

'Thanks,' he said.

Miles sat silent. He watched Gary Bones carry his rod and fish bucket and the shark tooth away. He watched him walk down the beach towards the bluff. He imagined him disappearing over the hill, imagined the tooth gone forever. Suddenly Miles was running. He was up and sprinting, picking up speed as he hit wet sand. Then he launched himself into the thick back of Gary Bones.

Time went strange then.

He was on the sand and he felt the cold water run up his trousers, felt it soak right through and up onto his back. And there were hands on his shoulders, strong and gripping. Gary Bones's hands.

Miles turned his face away, looked out at the water and it seemed to glow purple and metallic in the sunlight as Gary Bones's huge forehead came crashing down.

The light was bright and blurred. Miles leant up on his elbows slowly, tried to focus, found Gary Bones standing there on the sand. He had something in his hands. A fishing rod.

'It's broken,' he said. 'My Dad's rod – it's broken.' And he looked all weird and small like a kid.

They must have landed on it when they fell. They must have busted it.

Miles got to his feet and his face pulsed and throbbed, felt swollen. When he wiped his nose with the back of his hand it stung like hell. Blood came away. It was there on the back of his hand.

He started walking backwards, small steps, but Gary Bones noticed. Gary Bones was coming. And Miles didn't know what to do so he just started talking, talking out loud about the tooth and how he'd found it in the seat and he didn't know whose it was, but he thought that maybe it had something to do with Mum. That maybe it was hers. And he thought that he should keep it because she was dead. Because she died. And he tried not to look at Gary

101

Bones while he talked. He tried to look at the ground, but Gary was standing so close. Miles could even hear him breathe.

And a fat knuckled fist dug into Miles's ribs. Stayed there.

'Who says I was gonna keep it? Who says?'

And Gary Bones stared hard into Miles, smiled a tight mean smile. But his fist moved away. He dropped the tooth on the sand.

'If you weren't such a little freak, I'd beat the crap out of you, Miles.'

He was still in the bathroom inspecting his face when he heard the van get back. His nose looked OK now, not bleeding so much, but it was his teeth he was worried about. His tongue had been playing with one, pushing it this way and that, and it felt loose. It definitely moved when he touched it. He parted his lips again to have another look. It was the little tooth just next to his big teeth – the front ones.

'What the fuck happened to your face?' Joe was standing behind him, looking at him in the mirror.

Miles turned around and pulled his top lip back even further. 'Do you think my tooth's gonna fall out?'

Joe put one hand under Miles's chin, lifted his head to the light.

'This one.' Miles marked the tooth out with his tongue.

Joe touched it gently with his finger. 'I think it's OK, but stop touching it. Stop moving it with your tongue. I'll get some ice.'

He let go of Miles's face, walked away to the kitchen, and now Harry was at the door looking in.

'I fell,' Miles said.

Harry didn't say anything. He just stood there in the doorway looking dumb with his mouth wide open. Miles pushed past him and followed Joe to the kitchen.

Joe gave him a handful of ice wrapped in an old tea towel and pushed him out onto the verandah. Miles held the cloth lightly against the side of his nose and it smelled thick with grease and oil and old cooked meat. Water dripped slowly from his hands and Miles watched the drops land on the old wide floorboards below. He watched the wood suck the water in.

And he could feel Joe standing near, just behind his back, almost touching. He could hear Joe waiting.

'I fell,' Miles said again.

Joe sighed and grabbed the tea towel of ice out of his hands. He went to walk away but Miles stopped him.

ARRETT

'I know what happened to Mum,' he said. 'You think I don't, but I do. I know she crashed the car on purpose. I know she wanted to die.'

Joe grabbed hold of him. Squeezed his arms hard.

'Why would you say that? Why would you even think that? Jesus Christ, Miles, it's not true.' He chucked the tea towel on the ground and the ice cubes flew across the boards. 'She had this thing, this condition – high blood pressure. She took medication for it. That day in the car her blood pressure got really high and she just had a heart attack. That's it. She just died. She just had a heart attack and crashed the car and bloody died.'

Joe pushed Miles away. He stormed into the kitchen and slammed the door. Out of the corner of his eye, Miles knew Harry was right there. That he'd seen everything and heard everything. But Miles didn't speak. He didn't say anything. He just closed his eyes and pretended that Harry wasn't there, that he couldn't hear him or feel him. That Harry didn't exist.

He put his hand in his pocket, clutched the tooth tightly in his hand, the sharp edges almost piercing his skin.

He knew that the tooth belonged to him. That it was his.

104

*H*arry got up. The clock in the kitchen said 9:20. God, he'd slept for ages, hadn't even heard Miles get up and go.

There was still no bread, but it was Wednesday. Milk got delivered on Monday, Wednesday and Friday, and sometimes Dad ordered bread when he remembered about it. Harry stuffed his feet into his gumboots and ran down the drive to the road. He opened the meat safe that hung on the wire fence. Just milk. He carried the two bottles back to the kitchen and poured himself a glass.

There was no one at George's by the time Harry got there. He waited for a while on the verandah, then he walked slowly down to the back of the property. He passed the veggie patch and the woodpile. He passed the smoke house but it wasn't being used. There was no smoke, no smell coming from it. He kept on walking and he found a shed he hadn't seen before. It was right in among the trees and it didn't have a door, just an opening, a wall missing. It was packed full of junk: rusted paint cans, an old lawn mower, a metal bath full of broken tiles and rubble. Harry didn't look too far inside because he knew there would be spiders around and not just huntsmen, but bad spiders, red-backs and those shiny black ones that hid in busted tractors and rusted cars and any metal that had been eaten away. He was careful not to touch anything. He stepped away and he heard a dog bark. Jake. The sound was coming from down towards the bay. Harry followed.

George was in his dark green waders down by the water's edge. The tide was way out and the place stunk of mud and slime. Jake leapt from the thin wooden jetty and ran around Harry's feet, licked his hands. George climbed down the ladder into his old wooden dinghy. He sat down and patted the seat next to him.

He wanted Harry to come.

And even Jake wasn't scared. He ran past Harry, jumped in the boat and perched himself right up at the tip of the bow.

'I get sick,' Harry said quietly.

The water was still, brown and silty and full of tannin from the river, but George would be going out deep, out past the heads where the swell took hold of you as soon as the engine stopped. Out there the water rocked and pulled and pushed you until your stomach turned over and your eyes rolled backwards and you felt like you might be dying.

'I can't go.'

Harry tried to smile but couldn't. Not really. And he couldn't look at George.

That first time, when he'd hung to the rails of Dad's boat so tightly that he couldn't feel his fingers or knuckles or even his arms and the cold spray sliced his face like stingers, Uncle Nick had told him to look at the horizon. And he'd tried, but it kept on moving up and down and everything was grey – the sky and the water both the same – and he threw up all down his jumper.

'I don't think you'll ever be a fisherman, Harry,' Uncle Nick had said. And everyone had laughed. Even Miles.

'I'll never be a fisherman,' Harry said, but it came out all high pitched and squeaky and he had to clear his throat and say it again.

George stood up and climbed back onto the jetty. He started unloading his lines and tackle box and buckets from the dinghy. Jake jumped out too.

'Aren't you going now?

George shrugged his shoulders and smiled. He sat down on the end of the jetty with Jake beside him.

Harry took a step onto the grey creaky boards. Then another. When he got to the end he sat near George.

'Sorry,' he said.

But George was occupied. He was screwing one of the rods together, fixing the line. He opened his tackle box and got out a brightly coloured yellow and orange plastic lure and a shiny silver hook.

'Flathead,' he said, and he handed the rod to Harry.

'I can't . . . I don't know what to do.'

George grabbed the rod, cast out quickly with a flick of his wrist, and handed it back to Harry.

Harry didn't want to lose George's rod, or break it or do anything embarrassing, so he grasped the handle tightly in his hands and shoved the base between his legs for backup. No one had ever taken him fishing. Not even Granddad or Joe or anyone. He'd seen people fishing – kids off the pier at Dover and Southport, men beach fishing in the surf at

Roaring at dawn and at dusk — but he couldn't do it. He knew he wouldn't be able to do it. And George was just humming, getting another line together. It was a low hum, a kind of song like singing with no words.

Maybe nothing would bite on that hook at the end of his line and he could just sit here and pretend to be fishing. That would be the best thing that could happen. And he said the words silently in his head: please fish just keep away. All you fish just keep away from my lure and that little silver hook.

Jake pushed his head between the two of them, put his cold wet nose on Harry's cheek, snorted and took a look around. Then he was off again, sniffing something in the river weeds. Harry knew that Jake could keep himself amused all day as long as George was somewhere nearby. He could be free if George was there watching over things.

George settled in beside him with his line cast out and he was still humming, just softly, and the clouds were moving in the sky. The breeze was just onshore, but not cold. Not wispy. Harry let his back curve down, relax, and his hands were steady now, not clasped so tight. And he thought, OK. This is OK.

And he nearly jumped right out of his skin. His reel began to spin, the line running in a blur and the rod slipped right through his hands. But George's hands were fast, ready, and he grabbed on. He jammed the reel. The line slowed, the rod bowed right down to the water. And Harry found that one of his hands was on the reel again, right over George's hand, and then he was holding the handle of the reel all on his own, gripping on. He was doing it, slowly moving the line back turn by turn. And that fish must be big because it tugged so hard.

Jake was back, his eyes keen on the water just waiting for that fish to rise. He was whining, ready to bark, ready to leap into the water.

One wind, two winds, three, and there it was: speckled slime brown, the colour of mud with bulging eyes too wide apart for its body. Huge fanning monster fins on either side of its cheeks. George scooped the fish up into a net and flopped it into a bucket of water. It lay on the bottom against the yellow plastic, gills opening – gills closing. It was disgusting.

'Flathead,' George said.

Harry didn't catch any more fish, but George did. Four. Harry was happy to hold onto his rod and look out at everything and listen to the songs George hummed. And he thought that maybe he even liked fishing. This kind, sitting on the land kind of fishing. Maybe this was why Joe and Miles liked it so much. And he knew that Granddad would have taken him. It was just that he was too little, too small to go when Granddad had been alive. And if Granddad hadn't died then he definitely would have taken Harry fishing, too. And it would have been good like this was.

Back at the house, George gutted and filleted the fish, set them to cook on a hot plate over the fire. With a bit of salt and a squeeze of lemon the fish smelled good as they sizzled. Harry watched in amazement as something that had been so ugly, the colour of mud, turned bright white as it cooked.

The flesh was firm and sweet and Harry had never tasted anything so delicious.

$\mathcal{D}$ad had left Miles to clean the boat and deal with the cannery again. Deal with the men in white plastic with blood and fish guts all over them. Men with sharp knives and no smiles, soaked in fluoro light. That's what it was like in the cannery, fish guts and blood. It stunk of warm fish skin and bleach. And everyone who worked there smelled like that, too. It didn't wash away. The fish oil soaked inside their skin and it stayed.

Most kids ended up working there. Miles knew them; kids from school who left before the end of Year Nine. But they didn't look like kids anymore. They were hard. Just big arm muscles and thick hands. Gutting and finning salmon from the salmon ponds, shucking the abalone and canning them. And

Dad said Miles would end up there if he didn't work hard. If they lost the boat.

It was already dark when Dad picked him up and he didn't say where he'd been. He just drove fast. Took corners fast and Miles had to hold onto the door to stay in his seat and not slide across and hit Dad.

Now that Martin was out of the way, Jeff was in Dad's ear all day telling him that they should start diving over at Acton Island or down the cape.

'Why are we wasting time? We can't compete with the big boats,' he'd say.

He talked about other places, too. All of them out of the fishing zone. And in the afternoons, Dad would go off in the ute with Jeff. Maybe somewhere down the coast where they could poach close to the shore without being seen. Under the high cliffs and rocks down where there were no roads. In the mornings there would be a few tubs of abalone already on the boat. Big fat abalone.

When they got to the straight, hard bit of road, Dad pushed the ute even faster. Miles looked up ahead and in the blackness, maybe two hundred metres off, were the huge headlights of a truck coming. Coming down. And Dad wasn't even on his side of the road. He was in the middle of the road like always. Driving right in the middle of the road.

Miles kept his eyes on the truck, on the headlights, maybe only one hundred metres away now. Then the lights went out.

The truck was gone. There was only the sound of the truck and the sound of the ute moving on the road in the dark.

Dad's face was blank. Miles went to say something, to yell out 'Pull over', but the truck was suddenly there, suddenly right on them. The full force of its horn filled the air and the night and the cabin. And Miles could feel how close the truck was. He could feel the centimetres between them.

And in the headlights of the ute, Miles saw it. A bull on its side being pushed by the truck, its hulking body covering the space where the headlights should have been. A massive bull. Miles could even see one of his horns.

The truck must have hit it on the road, must have hit it up where the lights had blacked out. And Miles didn't know how the truck hadn't hit them, too.

He looked up at Dad, his eyes still fixed ahead. Then he turned and watched the red tail-lights of the truck fly away into the night.

It hadn't even tried to slow down.

And neither had Dad.

*J*ake alternated between leading and following on the narrow track through the scrub and the ground was really wet here, wet from the river and wet from the rain. Harry had never been this way before. Not this far upstream. No one came up here really, but George seemed to know the way. And it looked like all this land had been cleared once. A long time ago. When the forest was cleared it never looked right when it grew back. It was missing bits. There was no moss or ferns or dark hardwood trees. Just tall scrappy gum trees and grasses and shrubs.

They climbed a small hill and from the top Harry could see the bigger blue hills in the distance. A sea of blue forest going on forever. But below, in the valley, the layout of the land was clear. There were paddocks, old wooden stump posts, old sheds. And as they got closer, Harry could see the blackened stone foundations of a building. A house. The brick chimney still standing but slightly crumpled on one side where bricks had fallen loose.

George put his backpack down, got out some hessian sacks and handed one to Harry. And Harry could smell them, the red apples sweet and bubbling, ripe to bursting. It didn't take long before his sack was heavy with them. He could only reach the low branches, but the old orchard was so overgrown, the trees weighted and full. Rotten fruit was thick on the ground. He'd better watch out for snakes because there would be rats around – he'd heard some scurrying before, and Jake was barking and running like mad. Chasing rats and taking bites of fallen apples. He had one in his mouth now and he brought it over. It was slimy and half rotten, but Harry took it anyway. He chucked it as far as he could and Jake leapt after it.

Harry looked up at George.

'Is this your place?' he asked suddenly.

George let his full sack rest down against the earth. He looked at Harry. 'Yes,' he said.

'Where you grew up?'

He nodded. He picked up the sack again.

It was time for lunch.

⌒

Harry had taken his jumper off while they were picking and he'd enjoyed the winter sun on his bare arms, but now that he was sitting down he was cold again. George lit a fire, poured some water from his flask into the billy. He got out some bread and, using a large rock as a cutting board, cut a few rough slices. Jake got up from where he was lying and moved closer to the food. There was butter and some smoked orange fish that looked sticky. It glistened like it had been varnished. Harry didn't like smoked fish but he didn't say anything. He didn't want to be rude.

He watched George put some butter on the bread then a thick slice of fish. Then he took an apple out of his pocket, cut some thin slices and laid them on top of the fish. Harry took the bread in his hands. He could smell the fish but he was hungry, so he closed his eyes and took a bite. It was salty but sweet, too, and with the apple and the butter it tasted good.

The water in the billy started bubbling. George added loose tea and took the billy off the fire using a stick. When the metal handle had cooled down a bit, he grabbed it in his hand and swung the billy from side to side with quick, sharp movements. He poured the black tea into the two white, chipped tin mugs and there was no loose tea in them. Not even one leaf.

There was no milk, but Harry didn't mind. The warm mug in his hand and the fire were making him feel good. Good and warm and tired. He looked around at the old farm. He had so many questions that he wanted to ask George, like why don't you live here instead of in a marshy paddock? And how did the fire start that burned down the house? But he only asked one question.

'Do you remember your mum and dad?'

George nodded his head slowly. He put his cup down and rolled up his sleeves. Harry saw for the first time that George's scars weren't just on his hands and face. The bubbled white and pink shiny skin went all the way up both arms.

'Sometimes I don't remember,' Harry said. 'Sometimes I can't remember Mum.'

He caught glimpses of her in his head, just a flash every now and then and he tried hard to hold onto them. But he wasn't sure he knew the lady in the photographs at home. He wasn't sure he knew her.

'Dad doesn't like me very much,' he said.

George finished his tea in one big gulp and put his cup down again next to Harry's on the dirt. And he squeezed Harry's shoulder. He told Harry all about Mum when she was young. What he remembered.

⌒

Back at the shack, George gave Harry a small bag of apples to take home, but Harry said no.

'Dad will ask me where I got 'em,' he said.

George put the bag down on the table. He took out two apples and slipped them into the pockets of Harry's parka.

On the way home, Harry took an apple out of his pocket and rubbed it against his pants. He took a bite. It was sweet and the juice ran down his chin. And it was good like sunshine. Like the inside of an apple pie. He was glad George had shown him the farm. The place he grew up.

He knew they were real friends now.

*A* car pulled up the driveway. A new car, dark blue and shiny.

Harry held onto the curtains, kept them tightly shut with just enough space for one of his eyes to see out of the window. A man and a woman got out of the car. They were wearing uniforms like police uniforms but they weren't police uniforms.

There was a knock on the door.

Harry stood still. They knocked again.

The door wasn't locked and if the man and the woman tried it, it would open and they would see him hiding by the curtains. He moved closer to the door.

'Yes,' he said.

'Officer Warne-Smith and Officer Taylor here. Are Mum or Dad at home?'

It was a woman's voice. Harry reached out and touched the door handle. He opened the door a tiny way and put his face through the crack. The woman was short with blonde hair and she looked quite nice. The man stood behind her and he was trying to see past Harry and into the house.

'My mum's dead,' Harry said.

The man and the woman looked at each other.

'Is your dad at home?' the woman asked.

Harry shook his head. He let the door fall open a bit wider.

'He's on the boat.'

The woman looked down at the folder she was carrying and she wrote something down.

'And that's Mr Curren? Mr Steven Curren?'

Harry nodded. Now the man was staring at him. He wasn't smiling.

'At home on your own?' he asked. 'How old are you?'

Harry looked down at the worn-out doormat encrusted with mud.

'My aunt's coming,' he said.

The woman tucked the folder under her arm.

'We need to speak to your dad. You say he's out on his boat?'

Then the man said, 'We're from Fisheries. Your

dad's licence is not valid. Unpaid fines and a long list of infringements. We need to speak with him.'

Harry could feel the man staring at him and he wanted to say that maybe he'd been wrong, that Dad might not be on the boat and he was probably up at the shops. But he couldn't make himself say anything. He just kept his eyes focussed on the doormat and waited for them to leave.

The woman said goodbye but the man didn't.

Harry shut the door. He heard the man say, 'What a shithole,' and he heard the car doors close. They must be from Huonville or maybe from Hobart.

From the window Harry watched them reverse down the drive. And he thought maybe he'd go out for a while.

At least until Miles got home.

Sometimes mist hung in the air, still and wet, and it wouldn't move or disintegrate or change all day because the heat from the sun wasn't strong enough. It would take the afternoon wind off the ocean to break it up. To chase it away.

Miles walked up to Granddad's house after work. There was a For Sale sign in the front paddock nailed to a fence post. And it was almost empty now, the house. Broken chairs and full green bin bags left on the verandah. An old phone book on the floor in the middle of the lounge, a chipped cup on the kitchen bench. All of Joe's stuff gone. But there were signs that they had been here. All of them.

Deep grooves in the floorboards in the hallways and near doors, soot in the fireplace, brown smoke stains on the mantelpiece. Harry's treasure hunt items left hanging from windows and resting on the sills.

Joe had told Harry he could choose three for the boat and that the rest had to go. But Harry hadn't chosen any pieces yet. He just kept walking around the empty house looking at them all. Sometimes he'd pick up a shell or a bone or something and hold it for a while. Sometimes he would say something like 'I found this at Cockle Creek' or 'Cuttlefish are smart'. But he always put the item back down again.

Miles found the old carved notches on the kitchen door: the marked heights of all of them. Of Mum and Aunty Jean. Harry and Joe. Miles ran his finger along the last marking for him. It was hard to believe he had ever been so small. He was smaller than Harry was now. He always thought he would live here one day.

He walked outside and opened the door to the workshop. The workbenches and metal lathe were still there, too heavy to move. And there were piles of collected wood stacked in the corner. Not wood for the fire, but good wood, supple wood full of oil. Granddad's wood.

Granddad had made beautiful things. He made wood glow and shine, and Miles was going to be just like him. He didn't want to just be a carpenter like

Joe. He didn't want to build houses and kitchens or fixtures on boats. He was going to make furniture. Good furniture. Just like Granddad.

Miles walked into the workshop. He picked up a small gnarled piece of king billy from the pile and he breathed it in. It smelled of the earth, even after all this time.

They stood among the destruction, smiling at the abundance. Myrtle, blackwood, king billy pine strewn, left behind. There for the taking.

A freshly logged coup.

'Jesus, Miles! Look at all that bloody wood.'

Miles could smell the wood, the pine, the earth. He looked around, rubbing his hands on his corduroy pants.

'What should we get?' he asked, and Granddad grinned.

'As much as we can load up – as much as we can bloody load up!'

They started filling the trailer, large pieces first. And Miles was actually helping for once, managing to carry some heavy timber by himself. There were a few good-sized logs, big enough for a coffee table or bedside cabinets. All the smaller bits were good for the lathe – chair legs, bowls, lamp stands. Miles found a big chunk of king billy dripping with sap. Billy was his favourite; the way it smelled sweet like honey, the pink flesh so tightly packed it was as strong as stone. And it was the best wood he knew. Something made of billy could last forever if you made it properly. If you worked the wood right.

'Maybe we'll find some huon,' he said, and Granddad winked.

'Used to be everywhere when I was a kid, you know.'

And Miles did know. When he closed his eyes he could see it. The huon pine growing soft and silent by the rivers. The trees reaching wide out of the dark valleys, so perfect. And they would never come back like that. Not even in a million years.

'Got your eye on a piece?' Granddad asked.

Miles nodded, but didn't point it out. He'd leave that till later. He knew Granddad would be surprised because it was just a small piece, and it wasn't billy. It was a soft bit of celery top, the grain bold and clear and ready to shine. He could see what it could be, how he would sculpt it on the lathe. And it would be for Joe. For the boat he was going to build.

Something just for luck.

Miles heard Joe's van pull up the drive and he put the old bit of billy he was holding back on the pile. He went outside.

He waved to Joe and he thought that whoever bought the house would probably think all that wood was just for the fire.

*M*iles watched Joe mark out huge arcs on the slate green lines. He was wild, moving so fast he was flying. But Miles couldn't move. He just stood still at the top of the cliff, hardly breathing, watching the water below churn and run. It was shit that Joe had brought him here. Southport Bluff was rocky and rippy, a steep heavy chunk of water that jacked up over black reef. People called it the Bone Yard, maybe because of all the old shipwrecks, or maybe because the reef could break your bones. Miles didn't know, but he'd seen Joe get smashed here before; pummelled by thick white water, dragged backwards over reef, had the skin on his hands and feet ripped away. And Joe was much bigger than he was.

He was just a kid. A baby. He was nothing.

The light was going. Soon it would be too late. Joe was leaving. Leaving. And Joe had yelled at him before, said that Miles was going to get stuck. Stuck working for Dad, stuck being responsible for Harry, stuck being responsible for everything. He'd said that Miles was always scared of the wrong things.

'I bet every bit of you is screaming on the inside, Miles.'

And it was. Miles could feel it. His jaw tight, his fists clenched, just standing there with his wetsuit on and his board under his arm. Just standing there like he was dead.

But he moved. He started running, skidding blindly down the steep rocky path. Unable to stop, too scared to stop. At the bottom he picked his way along the exposed reef until the cold water hit his feet. He threw himself off the edge of the world without even thinking. Without breathing. He just paddled with everything. And Joe was hooting and clapping, giving Miles the strength to paddle faster. He felt the lines punch hard underneath him, pick him up like he was just a leaf, a piece of seaweed. But he wasn't scared now. Not of this.

It was simple.

What he needed.

The rise and fall of the ocean breathing and someone out there who felt it too. Joe understood. He lived for this, for these moments when everything stops except your heart beating and time bends and ripples – moves past your eyes frame by frame and you feel beyond time and before time and no one can touch you.

When he reached the main break it was bigger, thicker than it had looked from up high on the cliff. The back of the wave almost as steep as the face so that the peaks and troughs were metres apart. But Miles kept his eyes on Joe's eyes. Kept his eyes fixed right on Joe.

This next line.

His.

This wave was going to take him whether he liked it or not. He turned. He waited for that feeling when the back of your board gets lifted. For the moment when you are collected. And his body knew how. It knew what to do, when to lean in, when to pull back. That drop rolling out fast.

Everything fell out of his mind. He could see it all now right in front of him, see the ridges, the curves. See the colour of the water as it moved in the fading light. It was time to do something. Time to make something of his own.

⌒

Getting changed, Joe and Miles were laughing at
nothing, laughing at everything. Joe couldn't find one
of his socks, and Miles got his wettie stuck on one
arm and he couldn't get it free. It was freezing and
windy, but Miles laughed so much his face hurt. He
still couldn't believe he had surfed Southport Bluff.
He'd done it, caught a few really big waves that were
well overhead. They were still running through him.

In the car with the headlights on, his body relaxed.
It was dead weight cradled in the bucket seat. But Joe
didn't start the car. His hands were on the steering
wheel, but they didn't move. He just sat there and
stared straight ahead.

'I thought I'd leave tomorrow,' he said after a while.

He looked at Miles. 'With more big swell coming,
if I don't leave now then it might be weeks before I
can get out across the strait.'

Miles couldn't think of anything to say. There was
nothing. Joe said it was probably best if he didn't see
Harry because he wouldn't be able to explain, and
that maybe Miles could explain it better. And the
whole time Joe looked weird and his eyes were wide
and red. He looked like he was scared.

'You can tell him for me. And tell him I'm coming back.'

Miles wanted to get out of the car. He wanted to get the feeling back that he'd had five minutes ago, and he couldn't look at Joe. He pushed his body as far away as he could so that he was jammed right up against the door with the handle pushing into his ribs. Joe's hands were still on the steering wheel. Squeezing the steering wheel.

Miles thought he might be crying.

'I just gotta get out of here,' he said.

It was quiet except for the sounds of Joe and Miles wanted to tell him to shut up. He wanted to ask him what he was crying for, what he had to cry about. He didn't have to live with Dad and work on the boat. He didn't have to look after Harry.

Joe didn't park in the drive. He pulled up on the side of the road with the house just in view. He left the engine on.

'What time are you going?'

Joe shrugged. 'Early I guess.'

And Miles knew in his guts that Joe was ready to go right now. That he would probably slip out tonight and that's what this afternoon had been about. He'd planned this whole thing. The surf. All of it.

Miles pulled the handle on the passenger door and opened it and Joe reached out and grabbed his arm.

'I'll be back, Miles. I will.'

Miles kicked the door open wider and swung his legs out.

'I'm only nineteen, Miles. I'm only nineteen.'

Miles shut the door. He walked up the drive and thought that when he was nineteen, Harry would be nearly fifteen and they could both be the hell away from here too. That's what he thought. But it felt like it would never really happen.

It felt like it would never come around for him.

*M*iles knew how to make corn beef hash, only there wasn't any corn beef. Plenty of potatoes, though.

'Do you want mashed potatoes, Harry?'

Harry was watching TV and he didn't turn around, but he said yes. Then he said, 'What else is there?'

Miles looked in the cupboard. Tomato sauce. A small tin of baked beans, dry pasta, an onion.

'Baked beans?'

Harry nodded.

The bright red peeler didn't work anymore. It had rusted solid and no one had ever bothered to throw it out. Miles picked it out of the drawer, touched the rusted blade with his finger. He could use a knife, and he got the sharpest one out, but then again the potatoes weren't too dirty. He could just scrub them and mash them with the skin on. No, Harry wouldn't eat that. He'd better peel them.

It was hard to cut close to the skin and he ended up losing quite a bit of potato. But there was enough. Potatoes were filling. When Mum used to take them up to Huonville market they would always get hot potatoes from the Potato Man. The little black metal oven full of steaming baked potatoes. One cut in half, with melted cheese and coleslaw and herbs and butter oozing down, would be more than enough. It would keep Miles warm all day. But they didn't have any cheese or butter or any of those other things. Just milk.

Miles put Harry's serve on a small plate so that it looked like there was more food. A small tin of beans didn't go very far and Miles was careful to split the food equally, even though he knew Harry wouldn't eat all of his.

Dark outside, but still early, they sat and ate their warm beans and mash. And Miles knew he would let Harry use the last of the milk for a cup of Milo later, and he knew that Harry would ask him about it just as soon as he finished his last mouthful of dinner.

And then Harry told Miles about the people who had come to the door. About Fisheries.

*M*iles and Harry had stayed out for as long as they could, stayed out past midnight until they were freezing, because Jeff and Dad had been drinking for two days. But now they were back in their room and Harry was busting for the loo.

'Just go out the window,' Miles whispered.

'I can't.'

'Why?'

Harry didn't answer. He got out of bed and started jiggling. He could never go to the toilet outside.

'But you'll have to go out through the lounge,' Miles said.

Apart from two small bedrooms, the brown house was only one room, a kitchen–lounge with a concrete bathroom tacked on. Harry looked terrified but he opened the door anyway and ducked out. Miles heard his feet hit the lino in the kitchen and Jeff and Dad hadn't stopped talking. Maybe they wouldn't notice. Miles got out of bed just in case. He waited by the door. He didn't hear the toilet flush, but the talking had stopped.

'It's the littlest retard.'

It was Jeff's voice.

Miles opened the bedroom door a few inches. All he could see was Jeff sitting in the armchair and the back of Harry and Dad must be on the couch.

'Have a drink, Harry,' Jeff said.

There was a bottle of Coke on the coffee table. There was never any Coke at home so Jeff must have brought it over.

'Go on. Have a drink.'

Harry must have thought Jeff was going to give him a glass of Coke because he said OK. Jeff picked up a bottle of Beam from beside his chair and started pouring. The glass was half full when he handed it to Harry.

'I meant Coke,' Harry said, and tried to give the glass back.

'You'll bloody drink it.' But it wasn't Jeff speaking now. It was Dad. And Jeff was laughing. His face all red and shiny and laughing.

'Drink it,' Dad said again.

Harry took a sip. He was coughing as he tried to put the glass down on the table, but Jeff stood up and took the glass out of Harry's hand. He grabbed Harry in a headlock, wrapped his thick arm around Harry's neck and pulled tight. And before Miles knew what he was doing he'd opened the door and run out into the lounge. He looked at Dad, all glazed over and puffy. Glassy eyes that gave no hope.

'Let him go. Leave him alone!' Miles said.

'Ah, the other retard.' Jeff turned his body towards Miles and dragged Harry with him. He was enjoying himself. Grinning at the attention and Harry couldn't move. His eyes were bloodshot, tears all down his cheeks. Jeff rammed the glass against Harry's mouth and forced his jaw open. The liquid poured in and Harry gasped and choked. Beam spilled down his chin. Miles had tasted Beam before. It must be burning Harry, his throat and his mouth, burning his eyes. And Jeff was still pouring, making Harry swallow by jerking his head around with his wrist and forearm.

Miles took a step and lunged into Jeff, but Jeff didn't budge an inch. He just kicked out and caught Miles's leg. Miles went down and his head cracked the edge of the coffee table. He lay on the worn carpet face down. It stunk of damp.

He had heard the sound of his head hitting the table, a dull wooden sound, but he hadn't felt it. Not yet. Thick liquid ran into his eye socket and he knew it must be blood. Then his fingers burned and he cried out. Jeff's boot was crushing his hand, the hard soles squashing his fingers into the carpet.

'Dad!' he yelled.

Nothing.

Miles strained his head around to see Jeff move the empty glass away from Harry's mouth. Harry struggled for breath. He looked sick. He was pale and his face glistened with sweat and sticky liquid. Then he was sick all down his chin and onto Jeff's hand and arm.

'Ah, fuck. Jesus Christ, you little pig.'

Jeff pushed Harry away, wiping the vomit off his arm with the back of Harry's saturated t-shirt.

Miles realised his hand was free and shot up. But now Dad was up, too. Up off the couch.

He stood, unsteady on his feet, looking at something in the distance. Then his focus found Miles. And he had the same look in his eye he had the night he busted Joe's arm, when Joe was thirteen and Miles was seven. The last night Joe ever spent in the brown house.

And Miles remembered what Dad had said that night. What he had said to Joe. 'You're just like him. You're just like him.' Then he threw Joe hard across the room and Joe hit the kitchen bench and there was a terrible crack. But Joe didn't make a sound. He didn't cry or wince or anything. He just looked back at Dad and said 'I'm glad'. And Miles remembered that he threw up on the floor when he looked at Joe's bent arm, and that Dad made Joe clean it up.

Miles looked down at the carpet now. There was blood where he'd fallen, drops of blood. And there were drops of blood near his feet. One fell while he was watching, then he heard Dad slump back down on the couch. Everything stopped and was quiet and even Jeff was sitting down now.

Miles grabbed Harry and they moved into the bedroom. He didn't have to ask Harry to do anything, he was already changing his t-shirt and had his shoes on.

'I've got your jacket,' he whispered to Harry, and Harry grabbed some things from under his bed.

It was still quiet in the lounge. Miles climbed out the window then helped Harry down. They started to run, not down the drive, but straight into the thick scrub at the back of the house. Then they heard Dad yelling from inside. Yelling at them, at everyone. Yelling at no one. And Miles could hear the words. They came through the brown walls, through the air and cracked open the night: 'I never wanted you.'

'Where are we going?' Harry asked.

Miles didn't know. Just somewhere away.

The thin track they were on disappeared when it hit the river and from there they had to skirt along the bank. They were careful not to get too close to the sides. It was dark. Really dark. No moon or stars, and it was hard to see the water. But it was there, rushing in the dark, catching on the edge debris and crack wattle.

'We could go to George's,' Harry said.

Miles stopped walking. 'What?'

'It's all right. George is all right. He knew Granddad and –'

'What are you talking about? How the hell do you know him?'

'I've been going over there to play with Jake.'

Miles grabbed Harry with both arms now.

'Who the hell is Jake? What are you talking about?'

'George lets me play with his puppy, Jake, and we have lunch. He told me all about Mum.'

Miles started walking again as fast as he could away from Harry, but Harry kept talking.

'He was friends with Granddad and it isn't true what people say about him and –'

'We're not going there, OK? I don't know him.'

They walked in silence for a while, Harry still behind Miles, until they got to the bridge.

'George is on the other side,' Harry said.

'I already told you, we're not going there.'

'Well, where are we going?'

Miles stopped. His eyes burned. He hadn't told Harry that Joe had gone.

'I don't know,' he mumbled. And he didn't know.

Harry stood beside him and put his hand on his shoulder. He kept saying 'We'll be all right. We'll be all right' and Miles didn't know how long they stood like that, but the cold had got in and he could feel it. He could feel something. Now his head hurt. It ached and stung and his right eye felt wrong. It wouldn't open properly.

'OK,' was all he said.

Harry led them across the road and onto a track, almost running.

*T*hey were close when a dog started barking from inside.

Miles stopped dead but Harry kept moving towards the small wooden shack.

'It's just Jake,' he said, without bothering to keep his voice down, and a light came on from inside. A figure stood in the half-opened doorway.

'It's me and Miles,' Harry said.

A dog bolted out the door and ran to Harry. It jumped around his feet and the man at the door waved them in. Harry went inside but Miles followed slowly. He stepped carefully onto the creaking verandah and he tried not to stare at the dark hollows and missing pieces of the man's face. Miles had never really seen George Fuller up close, had never seen his face, but somehow it didn't shock him now. Somehow the man standing there just looked like an old man. He was just an old man.

Miles turned away and stepped through the door. Inside a small gas lamp lit the room. The place was neat and ordered, clean, the walls painted white against the dark wood ceiling and supporting beams. There was a small bed against one wall, a table, one armchair and two wooden chairs, a single shelf with a few pots and things, a wood heater in the middle of the room, a rug, a metal trough with one tap attached to the wall. More things than Miles would have thought could fit in a place like this, and yet it all did.

George gestured for Miles to take the armchair, but he put his backpack on the table and sat on one of the small wooden chairs instead. Harry seemed happy to just stand there and not introduce Miles, so Miles didn't say anything either. He watched George fill an old kettle at the trough, the water from the tap running slowly, then he put the kettle on the wood heater. Harry fed the fire some more wood and sat on the floor with the dog in front of the fire like nothing had happened, like tonight hadn't happened and he'd always lived in this tiny wood shack with this old man. Miles looked at his backpack and then at the floor. His head really hurt now and the heat of the room was making his eye swell up. He could feel it growing, his eyelid fat and heavy. He cleared his throat.

Harry turned around.

'This is Miles,' he said.

The dog looked up at Miles for a second, then put his head back down on Harry's lap. Miles thought he should say something but he couldn't think of anything. George stood up and got a box down from the shelf. He put it on the table and pulled out a bottle of Dettol and a cloth.

'OK?' he said, and the sound came from deep in his throat and nose, rather than out of his mouth. He pointed at the cut on Miles's forehead. Miles nodded.

George diluted some of the Dettol with water and soaked the corner of a cloth in the liquid. He moved towards Miles, touching his forehead lightly. He brushed the hair away from the wound and dabbed gently at the cut. The antiseptic stung the broken skin and Miles pulled away. There was blood on the cloth, bright and fresh. Miles breathed in.

'You OK?' Harry asked, and Miles nodded.

George fished around in the box and found a butterfly clip. He squeezed the skin tight and applied the bandage, then put blobs of some kind of cream around Miles's eye and cheek. It was cold and it smelled like Aunty Jean's herbal tea, but it made his head feel better.

The kettle boiled. George poured some tea into a teapot, followed by the hot water. There were two teacups and one mug. George went outside to the verandah and came back with a bottle of milk. He poured it in all three cups and put the bottle on the table. Miles stood up, having a purpose, and took the bottle in his hand. George nodded. It was really warm inside now and wouldn't take long for the milk to go bad.

He could see quite well on the verandah because of the light coming though the window, but the moon was still behind clouds. There was a meat safe hanging from the roof and below it a wooden cupboard with flywire sides. Miles put the milk in the otherwise empty cupboard and went back inside.

A cup of tea was waiting for him on the table. Harry had the other cup in his hands.

'George put the sugar in already. I told him you have it like me.'

Miles looked at George as he sat down on the chair again. 'Thanks,' he said.

Harry gulped his tea down like it was a cold drink. Joe always added some tap water to Harry's tea when he wasn't looking because he always gulped it down, no matter how hot it was. He got up off the floor and put his empty cup on the table.

'These are like Mum's cups,' he said.

Miles looked at the cup in his hand. It was like the ones Mum liked, like the ones she had. Aunty Jean had taken all the cups away after she died. She said Harry and Miles would just break them if she left them at the house. Now they were displayed in a glass cabinet at Aunty Jean's and they were never used for tea. They were never used for anything.

'If you need to go to the loo, it's outside. I'll show you where it is if you want,' Harry said.

Miles watched George go over to a cupboard and get out a pillow, a sleeping bag and a rolled-up sleeping mat. Harry helped him unroll the mat on the floor and unzip the sleeping bag so that it opened out to double size like a doona. They seemed to have an understanding, George and Harry. One that didn't need words.

'We have to share,' Harry said.

Miles didn't care. The sleeping bag in front of the fire looked good. It was warm and the light was low and now he just felt heavy and tired. He just wanted to close his eyes.

George sat down in the armchair.

Miles lay on the floor next to Harry under the sleeping bag and the dog burrowed in between them. He patted and cuddled the dog, felt its small heart beat into his hand, and wondered how it was that George came to live here in a wooden shack with no power and not much of anything.

Harry's breathing changed. Miles guessed he was asleep already. The gas lamp went off and soft, warm light filled the room. Miles heard a match strike. He watched the flame, watched George light his pipe and the smell washed over him. He closed his eyes. He knew that smell. It was the smell of Granddad's house, the smell of rich sweet pipe tobacco. And Miles could see Granddad sitting by the fire listening to the radio, his eyes almost closed, slowly puffing on his pipe. And he was there, too. Just a small boy, playing on the floor with his Matchbox cars.

*G*randdad had made him a toolbox.

And he'd watched Granddad make it. He'd tried to help. He'd handed Granddad things when he needed them. The plane. A chisel. The four screws that held the whole box together. And Granddad had carved his name carefully on the side, M. Curren in curly writing.

Granddad said Miles would be old enough to have some tools of his own soon. Old enough when he was five. And he held on tightly to the handle of his toolbox when Mum came to pick him up. He cradled it on his lap and waved goodbye as they reversed down the drive.

It was getting dark. When they got on the road, the radio crackled with some old kind of song and a man was singing low and soft like sleep. And with the sound of the car and the sound of the radio and with Mum's voice softly singing along, Miles had to close his eyes. He had to rest his head down against the window.

But the car stopped.

Miles lifted his head, blinked his eyes. They weren't at home. They were still on the road. On the road near the bend where the track was narrow and dark, and Mum opened the door. She got out of the car and left the door open and the cold air rushed in. Miles called out, but she was already into the trees and she didn't hear, or at least she didn't stop. She just walked into the darkness and was barely there to see at all except the white frill on the bottom of her skirt that flashed as she moved.

Miles opened the passenger door. He got out of the car and he stood on the road.

'Mum?' he said, and he looked into the trees.

Now he couldn't see her at all.

He stepped onto the earth covered with leaves and cracking sticks and he touched the rough trees with his hands. The wind rustled high above, invisible, and made the air rain leaves. They fell on his face. He kept on walking. He kept on going deeper into the forest until he saw her, almost see-through in the dark. Just an outline now. Mum leaning against a tree, her arms hugging her sides. And she was crying.

Miles stood silent until he could barely see her anymore, and then he asked quietly if they could go home.

And her voice was small, but he heard her. A whisper.

'I left here once. But I came back.'

Miles moved closer. He felt for her hand.

'My darling,' she said.

And he led her back through the trees, and back to the car and her skin was like ice.

Miles rolled over and opened his eyes.

Harry was there next to him on the floor, fast asleep. He sat up. George wasn't in the room. His bed was made, neat and tidy, and maybe he'd never slept in it at all. Miles had seen him there, his dark silhouette still in the armchair. But then he'd closed his eyes. He'd slept like stone. And he didn't know how the night had passed or how long he'd slept. He just remembered feeling the warmth of the dog on his back and then there was nothing.

It must have been because of his head.

He touched the cut with his fingers, traced over the butterfly clip. The lump around it was hard as bone, but his eyelid opened properly. His eye was working. He could see that the light coming in the window was mid-morning light. They had slept late.

He slid from under the sleeping bag and stood up. The air was still warm in the little room, warm from the wood heater, but through the window he could see that the sky outside was clear and cold. He put his jumper on and opened the door.

George wasn't outside; neither was the dog anywhere that he could see. The outhouse was down the back of the paddock and he walked there in bare feet. The earth was cold and damp like always, but at least it wasn't muddy.

He knocked on the door of the toilet just in case George was in there, but he wasn't.

When Miles got back, Harry was sitting at the table eating a slice of bread and butter.

'Your eye looks bad,' he said, and he pushed a plate of bread over towards Miles.

Miles sat down. It looked good, the bread, thick and dark and homemade. But he didn't touch it.

'It's not our food,' he said. Harry just stared at him and kept eating.

Miles looked at all the things on the table. Bread, a jar of honey, butter on a small plate.

'Did you get the butter out of the cool box?'

Harry shook his head. He got up from the table and walked outside. He came back in with the milk, but it wasn't the bottle from last night. It was a full bottle. He poured himself a glass.

Miles tried to think where George would get his milk delivered. He had never seen a cool box on the road near the property, and there was no driveway. He wondered how George managed with the other groceries, too. Maybe he got a delivery from Dover. Miles wished that Dad would do that so they would know when food was coming and how long they had to make things last.

Harry finished his milk, wiped his mouth with the back of his hand, and Miles gave in. It was the smell of the bread and the smell of the butter.

He held a piece in his hands and took a bite.

Miles got up and rolled the bedding. He put the mat, pillows and sleeping bag back in the cupboard and Harry didn't help him. He just watched from where he was sitting at the table.

'We'd better get going,' Miles said, but Harry stayed where he was. He played with the butter knife, then he put it down on his plate.

Miles walked over and swept the crumbs off the table with his hand.

'We can't stay here, Harry,' he said.

But Harry didn't look up at Miles.

'George wouldn't mind. He'll be back soon.'

Miles shook his head. He walked over to his shoes and put them on.

'I'm going now,' he said, and he paused at the door, looked back into the room. Harry was still sitting at the table with his head down.

'Joe's gone, isn't he?' Harry said quietly.

Miles heard him but he didn't answer. He couldn't.

*H*arry put the milk back in the cool box, shut the door and ran.

Miles was already all the way across the front paddock and Harry didn't catch him until they were up near the road. When they stopped, he tried to ask where they were going, but Miles held up his hand to keep him quiet.

Harry shut his mouth. He watched Miles looking up and down the road. Listening. Harry couldn't hear any cars or trucks, he could only hear his heart beating in his head. He took a few breaths.

'Where are we going?' he said.

But Miles didn't answer. He just walked out into the middle of the road then headed into the scrub on the other side. Harry followed, but there was no path and branches flicked in his face and his feet slipped on all the sticks and leaves and wet earth. Miles was way ahead, blending in with the grey of the trees and the grey of the sky and soon he would be gone completely.

So Harry stopped walking. He stopped and stood still and he waited.

He counted in his head. And he heard Miles crashing back through the bush, cracking sticks with his hands and with his feet, and he thought Miles would be angry. But he wasn't. He was pale. He talked quietly.

'I'm taking you to Stuart's,' he said.

Harry looked at him. This wasn't the way to Stuart's. This was the worst way they could have gone because they'd have to bush-bash and cross fences and go across private land. But he didn't say that. He didn't say anything.

It was because of Dad. Miles was scared.

Harry walked faster now. He stayed close to Miles, kept up.

Joe had really gone. He hadn't even said goodbye.

Stuart's mum was in her dressing-gown. She stared at the lump above Miles's eye and Miles said that he'd hit his head on the boat. Stuart pushed past his mum and stood in the doorway. He smiled at Harry and there was warm air coming from inside the caravan. Harry could feel it on his face. He was glad he was here now and he wanted to go inside.

But he knew Miles wouldn't stay.

'I'll bring you some clothes later,' Miles said.

And it nearly made Harry cry now, the way Miles's eyelid was all purple and cut – the bruise on the side of his face coming up bad. He put his hand in his pocket and felt for the sock that held his leftover money. He pulled it out.

'You should take this,' he said. 'You might need it.'

Miles shook his head. 'You keep it,' he said and he tried to smile.

Harry watched Miles walk away. He watched him cross the paddock, walk into the scrub, and he kept on watching even after he had disappeared.

And maybe him and Stuart were playing down the back of the property, or helping Stuart's mum pick berries for the stall. Or maybe they were inside eating lunch and Miles never even knocked or made a sound, because Harry didn't see him come back. There was just the backpack with some clothes left by the door of the caravan and, inside, near the top, were some chocolates and the bright orange dart gun from his Bertie Beetle show bag.

*M*iles walked slowly now.

　　　　The earth was heavy with mud and in the pockets of old clearings, well away from the road, you could see where people had lived. Old foundations hiding in the knee-high weeds. Places where houses once stood.

A house. A farm. A family. A home. Hemmed in by forest and mountains and big cold sky. And none of it was any good.

This place.

Dad's ute was gone.

Miles stood in the lounge and it was silent, the house. It was dark. He opened up the curtains and the light caught all the particles of dust. Full ashtrays, empty bottles; and down on the floor the blood was still there on the carpet. If he used cold soapy water and scrubbed hard he'd probably be able to get it out.

A slice of sunlight hit his face. He put his hand out to block the light, but it wasn't coming from the window. It was coming off the metal photo frame on the sideboard. A ray of light. The photo of Mum.

Miles walked over and picked it up. She was wearing a summer dress with her long hair down. It was sunny. And he'd never noticed before, but behind her in the photo there were dunes. A familiar shape; and the sand was fine and white. It was Cloudy.

That day at Cloudy.

Uncle Nick rode a long board – the old kind, fat and slow, but he could make it move. Like running free on the water, working the small waves all the way from the point to the sand. Uncle Nick, fluid and silent in all that bright light.

'You ready?' he said.

And Miles knew he wanted to feel it.

What it was like.

So he lay on the front of that big board. Held on while the white water splashed up in his face, freezing, and he could see nothing but Nick's arms reaching out to scoop through the water again and again. He felt the board move up and over, up and over until they were out deep. Until they were out on the clear.

Nick helped him sit upright and tall on the nose of the board, and with his legs hanging over the sides he was brave. He looked down into the water. All the way to the bottom.

Ripples in the soft sand. Balls of loose seaweed flying free and weightless. The black rock and reef hiding thin beneath the sand.

'Safe here,' he said, Uncle Nick.

And when Miles looked up there was a line of water, long and straight and rolling. And it was coming.

Everything was silent then. There was only feeling. Rolling, rolling; and silent.

The pulse. It lifted them up gentle and slow. Lifted them high so they could see.

Then it let them loose. Left them behind. And time came back.

Miles turned his face towards the beach, followed the line with his eyes. He watched it rise up. Watched it crack and peel, perfect, to the shore.

And he saw Mum standing there on the sand all golden in the sun.

He waved to her.

And she waved back.

Miles put the photo down, and he turned the TV on to break the silence. He'd better get started and clean the house.

He cleaned everything.

*M*iles could smell the fish and chips before Dad opened the front door. He walked in and put the greasy paper parcel down on the kitchen bench. Miles stayed where he was near the couch.

'Harry's staying at Stuart's,' he said, but Dad didn't look at him. He just got the tomato sauce out of the cupboard. He opened the fridge and looked inside, but there was no beer. Jeff and him had drunk it all. He stood up straight, shut the fridge door.

'There's potato cakes as well,' he said.

Miles walked over and served himself some chips and a potato cake. There was a piece of grilled fish under them as well as two pieces of battered flake. He didn't know whether he should take the grilled piece of fish. Dad never got him grilled fish. It was too expensive. Miles usually just got chips and sometimes potato cakes because he never ate flake. Even the smell of it made him sick. It was bad luck to eat shark.

'It's grenadier,' Dad said, but he still didn't look at Miles. At the bandage on his head, at his eye.

Miles slid the fish onto his plate. He sat down on the couch, started eating chips, and Dad came over. He turned the TV on and stood in front of it. The news was on but the volume was down. There was footage of a car crash on the Tasman Bridge and traffic banked up on both sides of the road. One of the cars was pinned up against the railings, squashed in half.

'No chance they survived that,' Dad said.

He turned the volume up then sat down in his chair. 'I've been tuning the boat,' he said.

Miles looked at his plate and chewed a mouthful of fish. It was soft and didn't taste of much except salt and oil, but he ate it all and he ate all his chips and the potato cake. Then Dad asked him if he wanted more and he said no. He sat there holding his empty plate and they watched *Sale of the Century*. Miles didn't know the answers to any of the questions and a blonde woman in a blue shiny blouse won the game by thirty points. The prize at the end was a baby grand piano. She didn't take the piano. She decided to come back and play again tomorrow.

'Engine's sounding good. We'll be right for the morning,' Dad said.

Miles sat there for a while, then he got up. He took his plate to the kitchen and rinsed it in the sink, stood there with a tea towel in his hands. He wanted to ask about Fisheries, about Dad's licence. But he didn't. With Harry gone for a few days maybe it would be OK. Maybe Dad would be OK. He dried the plate and put it back in the cupboard.

'See you in the morning,' he said, and he walked into the bedroom.

*A* girl with a round face and yellow hair leant against the wall of the rusty bus shelter next to the shop. Harry didn't know her, hadn't seen her before, but that didn't mean anything. He hardly knew anyone. It was windy, but she only had bare legs, and they were blotchy and purple and her short skirt looked too tight. She rubbed at her legs with her chubby hands, all the while looking down the road. It was past nine. Maybe she'd missed the bus. Maybe the bus was late. There was only one. If you missed it, there wasn't another.

'What do you think you're look'n' at?'

Harry stood still. He didn't know what to do, but Stuart pulled at his sleeve, dragged him forward towards the shop.

'That's Robbie Pullman's sister,' Stuart said. 'She's a fat bitch.'

He must have said the last bit too loudly because his mum turned around and gave them both a look. She didn't say anything though. Stuart's mum didn't talk much.

Inside the shop, Harry and Stuart looked at the poster of all the different ice-creams. Harry could feel all the coins in his pocket. There were a few notes in there, too. He could buy them both an ice-cream if Stuart's mum didn't mind. Stuart moved away after a bit and joined his mum who was busy filling a wire basket with tins and groceries from the two small aisles, but Harry stayed where he was. He kept looking at the pictures.

Bubble O' Bill, Eskimo Pie, Splice. It wouldn't cost much to get two Bubble O' Bills.

Harry could smell the hot chips that had just been dumped into the bain-marie. He turned and Mrs Martin was looking right at him. Watching him. All the kids hated her. Sometimes she locked the door so kids from school couldn't get in while they waited for the bus. Some of the older boys called her 'troll' through the windows, but she knew all their names, knew who they were.

'I'll tell your parents,' she'd yell out, and the boys would just laugh at her and throw stones at the glass. Harry and Miles never had any money so they never had to worry about Mrs Martin shutting the shop or not shutting the shop. Harry only ever came in here with Aunty Jean, or Stuart's mum. Even so, Harry thought that Mrs Martin probably knew his name, too, and knew Dad.

He moved away from the ice-creams and stood behind a shelf so Mrs Martin couldn't watch him anymore. There were jars of instant coffee and sugar and cans of condensed milk and tea on the shelf. There were all different kinds of tea bags in boxes. All different kinds. And there was one shiny black tin with silver writing on it that said English Breakfast. It was the loose tea, the kind George liked. Harry picked it up. The price at the bottom said $3.25. It was nearly all the money he had left.

Stuart's mum had paid and she and Stuart were waiting for Harry by the door. Harry walked over and put the tin on the counter, but Mrs Martin ignored him and stayed near the bain-marie.

'I'll buy this, please,' Harry said, and he looked right at Mrs Martin, but she still didn't move.

Stuart's mum came over.

'Harry, if you need tea at home, I'll get it. But your dad would use tea bags. We'll put this one back.'

Harry pulled the money out of his pocket and put it on the counter. He looked up at Stuart's mum. 'I need this one. It's for Aunty Jean.'

Stuart's mum didn't say anything else but she stayed near him, and Mrs Martin came over, started counting the money on the counter.

'I'll get two twenty-cent bags of mixed lollies as well,' Harry said, and he smiled at Stuart. Stuart smiled back.

The girl was still there by the bus shelter when they left the shop. She was smoking a cigarette now, still looking down the road. She had definitely missed the bus. As they drove off in the car, Harry turned and looked through the back window. The girl chucked her cigarette on the gravel and kicked at it with her foot. Then she kicked the bus shelter.

She was stuck here, too.

'You can drop me off near the bridge.'

It would save him having to walk all the way to George's from home, only he regretted saying anything now. He could see Stuart's mum's eyes in the rear-vision mirror and she looked worried, like she was about to ask a question.

'Aren't you coming back to ours?' Stuart said.

Harry shrugged. He felt bad. Stuart was nice and staying there was good except that they had to sleep in the annex of the caravan and the air was a bit cold on your face. But Stuart's mum always put hot water bottles in their beds so that the sheets and doona were already warm when you got in. So warm you couldn't help but go straight to sleep, even if you didn't want to, even if you wanted to stay up talking.

Harry put his hand in his pocket, felt for his dart gun and pulled it out.

'You can take this. You can keep it till I come and stay again.'

Stuart took the orange plastic gun in his hands.

'When?'

'Maybe tomorrow, or the next day? Don't lose the darts.'

Stuart nodded. He took the darts from Harry's hand and put them in his pocket. Harry knew Stuart would lose at least one.

Near the bridge the car pulled over. Stuart's mum turned. She looked right at Harry, held onto the seat with her arm.

'Maybe you should come home with us, sweetie. I'll make some lunch later.'

'There's food at home. Dad will have left something out. Thanks for having me, Mrs Phillips.'

Her eyes were big, but she didn't say anything else.

Harry got out of the car and shut the door. He waved to Stuart and Stuart waved back. And Harry kept waving, hoping the car would drive away. But it didn't. Stuart's mum was taking ages. She was worrying, having one of her moments where nothing happened and she just went still for a bit. Went quiet. Dad said she was cracked, but Harry thought she was nice. She was just nice.

Finally the car pulled off. Slowly. Stuart turned in his seat and pulled a funny face and waved again with the dart gun firmly in his hand. Harry coughed in the dust, waved one last time. When they were gone, he ran down the road to the path that led to George's, clutching the tea.

*H*arry knew it now — every step, every tree, and the tea in his hands shook inside the tin, a hollow metal ring with each step. He couldn't wait to give it to George. They would have tea and sandwiches and sit down and it would be warm in the shack. Jake would be excited, then he'd settle down and fall asleep right on Harry's feet like he always did. But where was Jake? Usually he'd run up to meet Harry by now. Jake could always hear Harry coming long before he reached the shack, and the shack was in view now. No smoke coming from the chimney. No Jake anywhere.

Harry kept running anyway, all the way to the door.

It fell open, silent.

He stood there out of breath, his heart beating, and the place was so still — so quiet. It felt like it had been empty for a long time, empty for years and years. And it felt like it would be empty forever. Looking into that dark quiet room Harry thought he might never see George or Jake again.

The metal tin felt cold in his hand. He heard the wind rustle in the trees and he had a feeling in him like he wanted to run. To run and run, to keep on going until he found George and Jake. And when he did, he would beg them to take him with them, wherever they were going.

But George's pipe was right there on the table. And his clothes were still hanging up. His pots and pans, his billy. Jake's blanket there on the floor. Harry was just being silly. They would come back. They were probably just out walking somewhere or fishing. And Harry bet that if he ran down to the jetty, George's dinghy would be gone and they'd be back soon.

Harry put the tea down by the door and headed straight for the wood shed. He found George's axe wedged in a thick round stump, but he wouldn't need to use it. There were high piles of dry kindling stacked neatly and lots of bigger logs, too. George was good at chopping wood. Harry was good at chopping wood if he got to use the blockbuster, but Miles hardly ever let him use the blockbuster. He said it was too heavy for Harry and that he hit the concrete more times than he hit the wood. Miles made Harry use the hatchet. The hatchet was stupid. It was small and light and you couldn't get any momentum. You had to whack the wood so hard that it hurt your arm all the way up like lightning when it struck the log, and if you missed the grain, if the hatchet came down wrong, then the wedge got jammed and the whole bloody log would be stuck to the end of the hatchet and you couldn't get it off. That happened nearly every time Harry cut kindling with the hatchet. Then Miles would say 'Leave it Harry, I'll do it', and he'd look disappointed and Harry would just stand there, useless, and watch Miles sweat and grunt and bust logs with the blockbuster.

Harry piled kindling in his arms, cradling as much as he could, and he took it inside and dumped it in the metal bucket next to the wood heater. He knelt down by the fire and scrunched newspaper up into tight little balls. The tighter you scrunched, the longer it lasted, but you had to leave one corner flat so that the flame would catch the paper. He built a triangle of kindling, giving it space to breathe, and he swept the floor clean with a dustpan and brush. He put the tea on the table and sat down on a chair. Then he waited.

Anyway, it was still quite early, maybe past lunch, but not too much past. The sun was still clear and high, even though it didn't warm anything up much. Harry had forgotten to bring his parka. He must have left it in Stuart's mum's car. But he'd start the fire just as soon as he heard them coming. It wouldn't be long. Jake would come in first. He'd come running and Harry would hear his nails *chip-chipping* on the verandah and then feel Jake's cold nose pressed right up against his hand. George would be way back, carrying all the gear – the lines and buckets of flathead or salmon or squid, and Harry would go to meet him as soon as he'd lit the fire and he'd help him carry the buckets or whatever was needed.

Harry reached over and grabbed the small folded blanket from the end of George's bed and put it over his legs. Lunch would be good – fish, if George had caught any. He pulled the bag of mixed lollies out of his pocket, fished out a bullet, a freckle and a raspberry to keep him going, then he twisted the paper bag closed and put it back in his pocket. Billy stared at him as he ate the lollies. Billy – George's brother – the man in the framed photograph on the table standing up tall and straight and smiling in his uniform.

George had told Harry about Billy. About how he'd gone to war and how he'd gone missing and about how he'd never come home. And Harry had thought about it quite a lot. He'd even walked into town on his own and looked at the old war memorial to see if Billy's name was there. But he didn't tell George about it because he didn't know what to say.

All those names carved in the old stone. Familiar names like Blackall and Bones, Bradley and Good. Three Donnellys all in a row. Roberts and Young and Nelson and Taylor. And there in the middle was Billy's name: Fuller, W. W for William, but George called him Billy. He'd been lost all that time ago and he never came home.

Harry leant his head back against the chair and thought that if Miles got lost, if Miles never came home, Harry's insides would go wrong and they might never come right again. If Miles got lost.

And he wished that Miles was here now.

And he wished that George would come back.

Then he must have fallen asleep because when he opened his eyes the light outside the window had changed. At first he thought that maybe it was just the clouds and perhaps it was going to rain, but when he got up and opened the door it wasn't the clouds or a storm. It was just late.

He had to go.

He took one last look around the room, the tea on the table, the fire all set, and he knew that when George got home he'd know that Harry had been here and left him the tea and set the fire, and he'd be glad. Harry shut the door. He ran up the paddock, he ran through the trees, and after looking back quickly one last time, he ran towards the road with the day slipping into darkness right behind him.

*M*iles was so tired in the ute. The sun was down but it wasn't quite dark yet, and Dad had the heater on for once, blowing up on one side of Miles's face. He put his hands in front of the vent, let them warm through.

Joe had been right. There was something coming. Miles had felt it in the water. Seen it. Swell coming in steady, the wind right on it, pushing. It was ground swell. Brand new and full of punch – days away from its peak. Joe would be lucky if he made it across the strait in time. It had even made Miles queasy, the way the boat rocked. The way the water rolled up under it. And he never got sick.

Hardly any boats had gone out but Dad didn't care. He made them stay out all day.

It was hard for Miles to focus on the road now. His eyes were so vacant that, even though they were open, it was like they were closed. He rested his head down against the cool window and his cheek and face vibrated with the buzz of the engine, the movement of the car on the road.

It was warm in the car. It was snug, with all the bags and clothes packed in around them and Miles looked at Harry. His eyes were heavy, falling into sleep, and Mum turned in her seat.

'Ready?' she said, and Miles could just see her smiling in the dark, see the white of her face. And he wanted to stay awake and listen to the songs on the radio, to be awake when they drove over the mountain so he could see the city, because Mum said the lights of Hobart were really something. She said you could see all the lights of the wharf and all the big tankers and ships. Ships that sailed to Antarctica and to Argentina and Scandinavia. Ships that were as big as factories.

But the road was windy and the headlights were soft and it was so warm. And he wanted to say, Wake me when we get there, but he forgot. And something pulled tight around his neck, around his chest, and all the bags were falling. All the bags were pushing him down.

There was a blast from a horn and Miles sat up.

It was Harry on the road. Harry standing there frozen, his arms out like he would be able to stop the ute. He'd just run straight out of the scrub. He'd just run out from George's place.

Miles wanted to scream but his body was flung against the door as the ute swung out and skidded on the loose gravel. He felt the brakes lock and his head flew forward, almost hit the dash. But they stopped. The ute stopped and stones rained down on the windscreen and tray like bullets.

Miles looked out the window but he couldn't see Harry. There was too much dust.

Dad got out of the ute and slammed the door.

'What the fuck are you doing?' he yelled.

Miles got his seatbelt off, opened the door. Dad had Harry by the front of his jumper and had lifted him up off the ground.

'Well?' he said, and he held Harry in so close that their faces were almost touching.

Harry didn't answer. He looked at Miles out of the corner of his eye.

Dad started shaking him.

'What were you doing on that man's land? What the fuck were you doing?'

'There's a dog and I . . . I went to see if I could play with it.'

Harry squeezed his eyes shut like he was waiting to be hit, but Dad didn't move. He just kept staring into Harry's face.

Everything went quiet then. Dad went quiet and the whole place went quiet like there was nothing. No wind, no rustling trees, no sound from the river. Just Dad holding Harry up off the ground. And his face was dead and his eyes were dead and Miles felt sick.

But then he let Harry go. He just put Harry down and he walked away. He walked away and got in the ute.

Miles rushed over.

'Are you OK?' he asked quietly, but Harry didn't say anything. He just sniffed and grabbed hold of Miles's arm. And both of them jumped when the sound of the engine cut through the air.

On the way home Miles sat in the middle and Harry pushed his body close to the door. Dad just drove. Silent. His face was still blank.

At home he made them eggs on toast and Harry and Miles sat at the kitchen bench while Dad watched TV. And even when Miles took Dad's plate so that he could do the washing up, Dad didn't say anything.

*H*arry looked out the bedroom window but it was too dark to see anything. He could only see the reflection of the room and the reflection of him standing there.

The curtains had fallen down a long time ago. He couldn't say exactly when they had fallen down, but nobody had ever bothered to put them back up. Harry didn't even know where they were now, whether they even existed at all anymore. And every time Aunty Jean came to get the washing she said that somebody had to do something about those curtains — somebody had to do something. But nobody ever did anything.

It was all right, though. Harry liked to be able to see outside as soon as he woke up. To see the sky.

Miles was taking ages washing the dishes and when he finally came in and closed the door he didn't look at Harry. He just walked over and sat on his bed.

Harry moved closer.

'He wasn't there,' he said. 'George wasn't there and I think he's been away since we stayed. The dishes were still in the sink. Maybe something has happened?'

'Why didn't you stay at Stuart's? I told you to stay there.'

Harry sat down on the bed next to Miles.

'Sorry,' he said.

He looked down at his feet. The hole in his right sneaker was so large now he could fit his big toe all the way through. He wiggled it and it poked out. Miles seemed to be looking at it as well.

'It was really rough today,' he said. 'I think it will be too rough to go out tomorrow.'

Harry jumped up off the bed. 'Maybe we can go and see if George is back,' he said.

Miles stared at him. He shook his head.

'You're lucky Dad didn't go crazy, Harry. You're lucky he doesn't know everything and that he believed you about the dog. You shouldn't be going down there, OK? You've just got to stay home.'

'But George is all right. You know him.'

'Harry . . .'

But Miles didn't say any more. Harry sat back down. He kicked off his sneakers and they bounced on the floor.

'Do you think George is OK?' he said after a while.

Miles nodded. 'Probably fishing down the coast, or Bruny or something,' he said.

Harry hadn't thought about that. There were heaps of fishing huts at Bruny and around the place and George was probably just at one of them for a few days. He probably did that all the time to get all the fish that he dried and smoked.

Harry looked up at Miles.

'OK,' he said. 'I'll stay home.'

*I*t was close tonight.

The thick black coming down as Harry lay tight in his bed afraid to move.

He blinked his eyes. He tried to find something there in the darkness.

The window.

The sky.

The dark blue that comes before the dawn.

Like a dream, the darkness rolled away. Soft light from the stars filled the room more and more. Stars clustered together like jewels in the sky.

And the world opened up. The colours came.

He hadn't seen them since he was young, since Mum, and he had forgotten about the lights in the sky. The coloured lights that pulsed and shone and breathed life across the dark plains. Endless. Close but nowhere. The green and yellow ripples of light. The Southern Lights.

And they stayed until he fell asleep.

*M*iles opened his eyes.

It was dark in the room. It felt like it was the middle of the night and that maybe he was just dreaming because there was a figure sitting at the end of Harry's bed.

'Get up,' it said.

It was Dad.

Miles got up, got dressed quickly, and Harry didn't wake. Miles turned the bedroom light off and closed the door and Dad was sitting in the lounge waiting for him. He asked where Harry was. Miles said he was asleep and Dad stood up and marched into the bedroom. He turned the light on, pulled the doona off the bed onto the floor and told Harry to get up.

Harry rubbed at his eyes. He looked around and squinted as Dad left the room.

'What's happening?' he said.

Miles didn't know. He didn't know what was happening.

'I think you have to come out with us today,' he said, and pulled some clothes out of the drawer. Some pants and a woollen jumper. A pair of socks. He told Harry to put them on quickly, to get his boots.

Harry's eyes were huge.

'I can't go on the boat,' he said. 'I can't. Please, Miles, go and tell him? Tell Dad?'

Miles heard the front door slam.

'Quick, Harry, just get dressed. It'll be OK. Make sure you put this jumper on and your parka. Bring a beanie.' He started walking to the kitchen to get something for them to eat in the car. He heard Harry start to cry.

'I left my parka at Stuart's,' he said.

Miles turned around. He took off his jacket and handed it to Harry.

'I think we'd better do what Dad says, Harry. I think we better go. It's because you were out on the road in the dark.'

'But you said it was going to be rough today. You said you didn't think the boat would be able to go out today.'

It was true. Miles could even hear the swell from here. He could hear the ocean.

'It'll be OK, Harry. You'll be with me, and if you stay out on the deck you won't get sick, I promise.' Miles reached into his jumper and took off the string hanging around his neck.

'You can wear this, OK?' Miles put the tooth in Harry's hands. 'You can keep it if you like. Now get dressed, quick.'

Harry stood there looking at the tooth in his hands, and he looked so young and small like no time had ever passed by since he was the baby in the room and Joe had told Miles to be nice to him and help Mum out. And Miles had thought he wouldn't like it. But Harry had a way about him. A way that made you promise to take care of him.

Outside it had started to rain and the wind was making the rain slice down through the air at a sharp angle so that the drops hit your skin like cold bits of gravel. Miles walked out to the ute and Harry lagged behind. He opened the door and got in, but Harry just stood at the door.

'Maybe I'll stay here, Dad,' he said and he poked his head inside the cabin.

Dad turned and stared at him and told him to get in the bloody car.

Harry got in quickly and shut the door.

They crossed the river and started out on the main road. It was still dark. Miles wondered how long Dad had been sitting there at the end of Harry's bed, how long he had been in the room.

Harry suddenly let out a loud hiccup. He covered his mouth with his hands and looked at Miles, but another hiccup escaped. Dad smashed the horn with his fist, a sudden high-pitched blast, and Harry let out a squeal.

'This is what happens when you don't do what you're told,' he said.

Miles felt Harry squeeze into him. Felt Harry's body tuck right in and he didn't make another sound.

Mr Roberts was on the wharf standing under one of the lights. It looked like he was staring right at Miles and Miles wanted to wave but he couldn't. Dad was right next to him. Jeff appeared out of the darkness.

'It's wild,' he said, maybe to Dad, but Dad didn't say anything back to him.

Miles helped Harry into the dinghy and held onto him on the way out to the boat. It was rough. After they'd passed the heads the boat was really moving. Invisible swell pushing in. And the wind was stronger, coming up from the south, full of ice.

They were inside a bubble of fluoro light slipping out into the darkness. Miles held Harry by the shoulders, made him sit down outside even though there was so much spray hitting the deck. And he sat next to him, told him to hold on to the pole and look out to the horizon as soon as it was light.

'I'll make you a cup of tea when we stop, OK?' he said.

The fluoro light that bounced off the deck made the skin on Harry's face glow ghostly blue. He nodded and Jeff must have been listening to them because he told Harry that if he got sick, he'd have to be tied up on the outside of the railings. He told Harry that he'd better hold on tight or he'd fall off and they'd never ever find him.

Miles squeezed Harry's arm and told him to look at the stars to take his mind off things, because out here, away from the land, it wasn't raining and there were no clouds. The moon was out, a tiny slither, and some of the brighter stars were still shining, but they were becoming translucent and starting to hide. It would be light soon.

And once the sun cracked orange, it came up quick.

It changed everything.

When Miles looked at the horizon he saw three shapes in the distance. They were heading out to the old islands. The Last Islands.

Black in outline, black in shape.

Black Witch, Flat Witch, Temple Rocks.

Rocks that stood alone in the middle of nothing, in the middle of endless ocean. Miles had never been this far out. Beyond here, what? Only a few clustered specks of black on the map where no one ever lived and where no one ever went.

Maatsuyker was the last island to reach out of the darkness.

The end of the earth.

Out here the pulse could get bigger than ten metres and the islands were marked and scarred. Battered cliffs, broken rocky beaches, caves worn well into the rock. It was like another world, roaring and squalling with life. Cliffs screaming with birds, with shearwaters and silver gulls, oystercatchers and storm-petrels. Patches of scrub and green clinging to any flat surface. And the water was really moving, deep channels carved between the islands. Silent currents.

Dad anchored the boat as far out of the wind as he could get, on the calmer side of Flat Witch. It was the smallest island, the flattest. It was just a baby compared with the others. The air pump was on, the boat steady as it could be in the water, and Dad and Jeff suited up.

They went down.

Miles got Harry a cup of tea and told him he could sit in the cabin now if he wanted to get out of the wind. But he didn't want to. He said he might get sick, so he stayed on deck close to Miles. He seemed OK. He wasn't green and he looked out at Flat Witch.

'That is where that lady is meant to have lived,' Miles said.

Harry looked up at him. 'What lady?'

'You know, the one who took off and went bush. Stayed out here.'

Harry shook his head. He mustn't have ever heard that story.

And it was only a story. That lady. The one who hitched a ride all the way down here with some bags of rice and a tent. Stayed here. Lived here all on her own. Everyone knew it was only a story. But now that Miles looked closely at the sheltered side of Flat Witch, he guessed you could do it, live here, because there was life out here. The surface of every water-level rock chock-full of mussels and probably wild oyster, too. And there would be plenty of small fish in the kelp beds, plenty of crays.

When it wasn't too windy – when the swell wasn't coming in crazy – it would be OK out here. You could live here.

'Where did she come from?' Harry asked.

Miles shrugged. He wasn't sure. 'Maybe the city,' he said.

'When was it?'

'Before we were born sometime. A long time ago.'

'And what happened? Did she stay? What happened?'

But Miles didn't know the end to the story. He didn't know what was meant to have happened to the lady.

'She decided she'd had enough after a while and she went back to the city,' Miles said.

Harry looked back at the island.

'How did she leave?' he asked.

Miles shook his head slowly. 'She must have seen a fishing boat and called them over or something.'

Harry looked like he was thinking about that. He looked like he was searching the island for clues.

'She must have just had enough of everything,' he said.

And Miles didn't know whether he meant had enough of life before the island, or life on the island. But there was a loud sound of metal screeching, the smell of smoke. Then there was the sound of nothing.

Miles stood still. Heat shot up his spine and ripped through his guts. The pumps had stopped. The engine had stopped. Dad and Jeff had no air.

He ran into the cabin, turned the engine over. Nothing. He tried again, but it wasn't even ticking over. He lifted up the floor, squatted down and ripped the metal cover off the engine. He heard his skin blister, felt the sting. The metal was red hot and it stuck to his skin. When he pulled his hand away his palm was raw. He closed his hand shut, bit down on his tongue. It must have been at least sixty seconds since the air pump had stopped.

He stood up and tried the engine again. Nothing.

He ran out on deck to the emergency generator to the air pump. It wouldn't start either. The fuel tank was empty. Miles looked over at Harry. He was still standing exactly where he had been, looking blank, his arms by his sides. There was nothing else Miles could do. Nothing.

He stood next to Harry and looked over the side – searched the moving water for bubbles of air. Cold trickles of sweat ran down his back and he thought that maybe he should just run. Get the hell off the boat and swim for the island, because if Dad and Jeff made it up alive, then he was dead. But he knew he would never make it, not with Harry. The current was too strong. If the boat wasn't anchored, it would be pulled along like it was just a stick on the river. It would get smashed up against the rocks. Like they would get smashed if they jumped over the side.

'Miles? Miles?'

Harry was pulling at his arm as Miles threw up over the side.

'It's Dad,' he said.

Somehow Miles managed to move, help Dad get Jeff on deck and there was blood coming out of his nose, out his ears. His eyes were open but only the whites showed.

Miles thought he might be dead. Maybe every drop of blood would pour out of him until there was none left.

Dad slumped down next to Jeff on the deck. He lay still and looked up at the sky. He took short breaths in and short breaths out. One of his eyes was trying to bulge out of its socket. It was bright red, filled with blood, and Miles couldn't stop looking at it.

'What did you do?' he said.

He tried to sit up and Miles took a step back. He could feel Harry right behind him. Feel Harry's hand on his arm.

'It just stopped,' he said. 'The engine – it just stopped.'

Dad stared at him, told him to get the oxygen and he ran towards the cabin but there wasn't any oxygen. They'd lost the tank with the mako; the first aid kit, too. He stood still by the cabin door.

Dad got to his feet. He stood unsteady as the boat rocked back and forth. The swell had picked up, maybe even as much as a few feet, and Miles could see the lines backed up high to the horizon. Coming in – pushing in with the wind.

'I tried to get it started,' Miles said, but Dad came at him, lurched at him, knocked him back against the rails so hard that his body bent over the side. His head fell back. It touched the water. And when the swell pushed in, he went under completely.

Into the cold.

Into the silence.

He opened his eyes, could see the water moving, and it felt like his whole head had smashed against the side of the boat because the cold stung so bad – the freezing water. His hands still held the rail but he couldn't pull himself up. Dad was too strong. Dad was holding him down.

Finally the swell rolled back and Miles could feel the air on his face. He sucked it in. Dad was staring down at him, his big hand tight around Miles's throat.

'That's what it feels like,' he said, and Miles kicked his legs, rocked his body from side to side, but it was no use.

He gasped and was under again.

It felt like longer this time. It was a long time. And when his breath was gone and there was just a burning tightness in his chest, his hands slipped loose from the rails, his arms fell back. He felt them touch the water, felt them floating free. And his head was light. His whole body light.

But something was pulling him, dragging him up through the water. And it was heavy, the water. It was holding him down. But he felt the air again on his skin, felt the world spin. And somehow he was standing, dizzy. Somehow he was on the deck.

He blinked his eyes, wiped his face with his frozen hand.

Harry was going mad.

He was punching Dad and screaming. Screaming, 'Let him up! Let him up!' and he was kicking Dad. Kicking his legs. And Dad was just standing there laughing like it was funny. Like it was a game. Harry kicked out again and caught Dad's ankle hard. Hard enough to make Dad wince. Then he looked at Miles and he ran.

And he was yelling, he was saying something over and over.

'We're at the Witches. The Witches . . . Please!'

He was on the radio. And his voice got louder and then he started to scream as Dad smashed into the cabin. Miles heard the radio receiver hit the ground before he could even move. Dad had Harry by the shoulders and he shook him like a rag doll. He dragged him out onto the deck.

'These are protected waters, you idiot! You always fuck everything up. You always fuck everything!'

And he slammed Harry against the rails. Held him there, and the spray was coming over thick now, soaking Harry, drenching his hair and running down his face. And Harry was squirming and moving and trying to get his body away from the edge until Dad pulled his hair so tight that he stopped.

Harry just closed his eyes then. He just shut his eyes.

And suddenly Jeff spluttered and coughed, and when Miles looked down he was on his side curled up, and he coughed again. He wasn't dead. But Dad didn't notice. He didn't even look. His eyes were fixed on Harry. He just kept staring at Harry. And his hand moved away from Harry's hair, moved down to the string around his neck. And he cupped it in his palm – the white pointer's tooth.

'It's his,' he said, and his face went pale. 'His.'

He let the tooth go. He stared down at Harry.

'She was leaving, because of him. Because of you.'

And that's when it happened. When something inside of Harry must have just gone wrong. Because he opened his eyes and he looked right at Dad and he said, 'I'm glad.'

And all of it came at once then.

Miles saw the wave; he saw Dad push Harry. And he went to run but something caught his leg, pulled him down. It was Jeff. Jeff right there next to him, all the blood drained from his face.

'For God sake,' he said.

And the whole boat tipped. A mountain of water broke the sides, swept the deck, and Miles smashed into the rails. He held on tight, held on until the boat straightened, until the water drained away.

But when he looked back there was only Dad.

Harry wasn't there. Harry wasn't anywhere.

*M*iles's mouth was open. His tongue moved but there was no sound, only the muffled crash of seconds passing: one, two. Then it came, a million seconds too late. His voice screaming out Harry's name.

Miles felt his blood as a fresh wave crashed against the boat. He climbed onto the rails, was ready to jump, but Dad grabbed him up – held him like stone.

And it was no good.

'HARRY!'

Miles saw Harry's arm reach out of the water. He saw his face there in the churning mess. The current had him now, his mouth open, his arms flailing. He was moving away, moving into the channel.

'You remember,' Dad said, and he held Miles tight. 'You remember, don't you?'

And he kept shaking Miles, kept pulling his face away from the water, away from Harry.

'They were dead when I found the car.'

And the insides of Miles went very still.

He couldn't see Harry now. He couldn't see him anywhere. There was only water. Only all that water moving.

'She was leaving me.'

Dad pulled Miles in close, so close that his face was all Miles could see. And it made him sick the way Dad's face was. The way he looked like he was crying. Like someone had done something terrible to him.

'I had to take him away, Miles. I had to leave you there. He was already dead and everyone would have found out. Everyone would have known.'

With everything he had left in him, Miles pushed. He pushed out his arms, braced his body back against the rail. And he screamed for Harry. He screamed his name out over and over. And he felt Dad move, felt his grip loosen.

'You're my son,' he said.

Then he let Miles go.

Miles took a step, grabbed onto the rail, and he looked back at Dad standing still with his eyes closed, his arms loose by his sides. Then he leapt into the water. He bombed down.

The cold wrapped him up, took his breath, but his feet kicked out hard and he pushed through the pulse. He opened his eyes, searched the surface, but there was nothing. He stretched his arms out, kicked harder. He swam into the channel and ducked down into the water. Through all the bubbles of air and light, somehow his hands found Harry, his body limp and floating free. Miles pulled them both up to the surface, but there was only chaos. Wind and noise – white water moving thick and heavy. They were right in the break. They were already right up against the rocks of Flat Witch, waves pounding down.

Miles held one arm out, Harry heavy in the other, and his hand scraped along the slimy surface of the rocks. But he couldn't grab onto anything. The water was too strong. His body hit the hard jagged rock again and again; sharp gnarls stabbed his back, his shoulders, the side of his head. All he could do was be a buffer between Harry and the wall. Harry lifeless in his arms, his eyes still closed. And he knew he wouldn't be able to get them out here, out onto land. He'd have to swim out deep, past the break. He'd have to get through the channel and try for another part of the island.

When there was a break in the push, he kicked off the rocks, moved towards the rising waves. As the first one hit, he grabbed hold of Harry's hair, gripping close to the scalp. He pulled Harry under and with his free hand he dug down. One stroke. Two. Three. The wave hit them hard and they began to tumble, flying like seaweed around and around in an endless circle. Surrounded by bubbles of air, the white of the churned water was all that Miles could see. He couldn't tell which way was up until the wave let go. Then the confusion dulled. Miles turned his eyes to the light and kicked until he broke the surface.

Harry was choking, coughing.

He was awake.

But white water was already cascading down the next mountain. Miles grabbed Harry's hair again but they were hit with such force that he lost his grip. He was alone in freefall, his chest on fire, his lungs empty. With both arms free, he made a desperate grab for the surface. One stroke. Two. Three. Four.

Air.

He couldn't see Harry anywhere, just water moving. Just water. He called out Harry's name but there was nothing.

This break in the swell would last thirty seconds at most. Waves came in sets and in this kind of surf, where the water suddenly hit shallow, you could get rogue waves. Bombs. Sometimes twice the size of the rest. On a board you could see them coming, lines that blocked out the sky and the sun. You paddled out wide or deep, out past the break. If you got caught, you bailed your board, dived as deep as you could, and prayed your leg rope would hold. And if you were lucky, the back of the swell just stroked you, pushed you round a bit, then you could come up for air. But ultimately it wasn't up to you. This ocean could hold you down for as long as it liked, and Miles knew it.

He called out again, yelling as hard as his body would let him and this time he saw an arm waving. Harry was bobbing about fifteen metres ahead. Miles swam towards him as fast as he could. There was a new set forming, growing stronger, and it was truly massive.

'Harry! Get behind me.'

'Miles!'

'Harry! Just get behind. Hold on!'

Harry could hardly clasp his hands together around Miles's neck. Miles told him to link his legs around his waist and Miles began to swim fast.

'Breathe!' he yelled.

He ducked them into the base of the next wave and it swallowed them whole. They managed to slip through, but the tail of the pulse pulled them back with it. Miles battled hard just to hold ground.

He felt like stone.

'Miles!'

Another wave. Harry was sobbing. 'Don't take me under. Don't . . . Please!'

Miles increased his kick, burst into freestyle. They started to move forward and met the unbroken face with as much speed as Miles could muster. He pushed into the steepness. If it started to crack, if the wave broke, they were gone. Miles reached as far as he could and with one big dig they were on the summit, the hump. He heard the wave snap and roar behind him but didn't look back.

They had made it past the break.

With deep, dark water beneath, they were set loose. Unanchored. They soared up rolling hills and down into the giant troughs. From what Miles could tell, the six foot they had been pounded with on the boat was steadily growing into storm size. Ten foot, maybe, the south-west wind giving it extra strength. And it was blowing enough spray to make salt rain.

And they were way past the islands now. The rocks and the reefs were gone.

There was no land at all.

Miles kept his legs beating at a slow pace, just enough to keep them afloat, and now that all the adrenaline was gone, he could feel the cold. The wind stung his face, his wet head. He knew the more you moved your limbs around, the more heat you lost. Blood moved to the surface where its warmth was stolen by the water. The key was keeping still. Slowing down. Trying not to fall asleep.

'I'm scared,' Harry said.

Miles didn't want Harry to know that he was scared, too. 'We just have to wait, Harry. We're OK.'

'What about sharks?'

Miles could hear the fear in Harry's voice. The tears.

'No sharks, Harry.'

It was exhausting to speak and hard to hear in the wind. Miles had to yell so that Harry could understand. He checked his own hands. Cut and scraped. Not blue, yet, but the water had started to feel warm against his skin.

Harry's crying eventually calmed, but Miles could feel his brother shiver. It was getting worse – rocking through his little frame like it was trying to keep his engine going.

'Harry? OK?'

'Is D-Dad . . . c-com-m-ing?' Harry's teeth were chattering like crazy.

'You got your jumper on, Harry?'

Silence.

'Harry?'

'Ti-ti-ger . . . win-ch-cheater.'

Miles swallowed hard. He'd told Harry to put on his woollen jumper. He'd left one out for him. He should have checked. He should have made sure.

'D-d-dad . . . c-c-om . . .' Harry could barely get the words out now.

No mate, Miles thought. No one's coming.

Miles wished he could see Harry properly, but knew he was better off on his back. Wrapped around. That way Miles could shelter Harry's head from the wind. If he took his jumper off and put it on Harry, it wouldn't make any difference. The heat trapped by the wool would be lost as soon as he peeled it away from his own skin.

'We'll be all right,' he said, and he closed his eyes.

He didn't know what to do.

There was a black emptiness inside him and it was all that he could see. He tried to imagine a fire in the darkness, and at first it was just one blue flame too small to feel. But he willed it on, felt the first flicker of warmth as it grew. Then it raged, turned into a ball of fire, orange and red and hungry. It devoured his stomach, moved up to his lungs, his back. Moved into his heart.

He shared it with Harry through his skin.

The flames hissed and popped, hungry for the new wood. Miles got into his pyjamas and Mum tucked him up in a blanket on the couch. She pretended to be mad with him for going near the river, but he knew she wasn't really mad. He hadn't meant to fall in. He'd just got too close to the edge and slipped and the current had taken him before he knew what was happening. It had sucked him down.

'It's just lucky your brother was there,' Mum said.

Miles looked up at Joe. He had fished Miles out and carried him home. He had saved him. He brought Miles over a hot Milo and Miles rested down into the couch.

'Warm enough, sweetheart?' Mum said.

'Yes,' he said. He felt the warmest he had ever felt.

'Don't go to sleep,' he heard Mum say, but it was soft and in the distance.

'Don't go to sleep.'

But his eyes were heavy. He was sinking down, into warmth, into light.

'Where's Harry?' It was Mum again, loud now. 'Where's my baby?'

Harry wasn't really a baby, he was three and a half, but Mum always called him her baby. And everyone thought Harry was so cute with his curly blond hair and blue eyes, but he just got in the way most of the time. He always followed Miles around saying, 'Whatcha doing, Miles? Whatcha doing?'

'Miles?'

It was a different voice. A small one.

'I'm not scared anymore.'

It was Harry. Miles could see him now. He was standing there in front of the fire. And he brought his face right down so that their foreheads touched.

Harry's big blue eyes were blurred by the closeness.

'I'm not scared of the water anymore!' he said. 'I'm not scared of the water!'

Miles was coming back through a fog. Wind against his skin.

Cold water splashed his face, forced his eyes open.

He spun around, frantic, and called out his brother's name. But Harry was gone.

*H*arry's feet hardly seemed to touch the ground as he followed Jake, and it was easy to run. He ran through the trees, reached out, and he could almost touch Jake's red fur. George was up ahead. George, waving from the top of the hill.

And when Harry got there, he could see it all.

The land just as it had been forever – untouched. Dark green tracks of forest over hills and mountains and rolling down valleys. Trees as far as he could see, running on and on to snow-capped peaks that lit up the sky. And there was water, too. Pockets of it and rivers of it. Big silent lakes of it. And he could see the ocean now. Light blue and dark blue. Places where the surface boiled up white and gold.

It went on for as far as he could see. The whole world.

And he thought, I am free – flying like a bird. I am free.

*M*iles was in the orange light that came before darkness. The sun burning brightly before it fell below the earth. He had been drifting for a lifetime and his mind had lost its way. It was dissolving and he had forgotten about Harry, forgotten about all the things that came before. There was only this vastness, the swing of a giant pendulum – water receding then flooding back. And he was part of it.

Part of the deep water, part of the waves. Part of the rocks and reefs along the shore.

He sank down in the water, muscles relaxed, no longer fighting. And he dropped away from the light and away from the air.

Ready now.

*W*ater spewed from his mouth, breath making him gasp and cough. He was being lifted, carried, his body swaying from side to side.

But his eyes were heavy.

The world was still too far out of reach.

He was thirsty. So thirsty. His lips cracked and stung. He felt a hand under his head, lifting it up and something cold touched his mouth. Water. He swallowed it down but now he felt cold. His body started to shake, to twitch. Pins and needles in his limbs moved down to his hands, his feet. Ripples of cold and feeling. He cried out and someone touched his head, stroked his hair. He still couldn't see.

He heard footsteps. Voices. The buzz of lights.

He fell into nothingness again.

It was Joe looking down at him. Joe.

'Thank God,' he said, and his face was weird. It was swollen and blurry and his eyes were thin, almost closed.

Miles looked around the room. He looked at the grey walls and door, at the low white ceiling. Uniform squares with hundreds of uniform holes in each. He was in the hospital.

He tried to sit up but his body wouldn't work. Only his head would move. Only his fingers. They stretched out and curled back, felt the sheet beneath him smooth and crisp and tucked tight. He made a fist and tried to hold it.

Joe reached out and touched his arm.

'I'm sorry,' he said. 'I'm so sorry.'

Miles opened his mouth to speak but no sound came. His throat was tight. He didn't know what Joe was talking about and now the hand touching his arm was hot. It was burning him.

'He looked peaceful, Miles. I mean, he was perfect. They found him on one of the reefs out near Acton and he was perfect. Nothing had touched him.'

Miles closed his eyes and tried to breathe.

He was in the water.

Harry was in the water!

He started screaming.

The sound bounced off the walls and off the floor and whipped around the room like a storm, but it didn't feel like it was coming from him. The sound was coming from somewhere else – from someone he could see.

A boy lying on a bed. A boy that couldn't be him.

The sound grew fainter, died away until it was nothing but a whisper he could barely hear. And he felt heavy and tired then. He felt warm.

It was warm in the car. It was snug, with all the bags and clothes packed in around them and Miles looked at Harry. His eyes were heavy, falling into sleep. But the car slowed down. It stopped, and Miles couldn't tell where they were on the road because it was so dark. He thought he could hear the river, but maybe it was just the wind in the trees. Maybe it was the ocean. And the passenger door opened and someone got in. A man.

'Ready?' he said, and Miles could just see Mum smiling in the dark, see the white of her face. And she said, 'Yes, my darling. Yes.'

And the man turned in his seat. He reached over and stroked Harry's cheek. He looked at Miles.

It was Uncle Nick.

And Miles wanted to stay awake and listen to the songs on the radio, to be awake when they drove over the mountain so he could see the city, because Mum said the lights of Hobart were really something. She said you could see all the lights of the wharf and all the big tankers and ships. Ships that sailed to Antarctica and to Argentina and Scandinavia. Ships that were as big as factories.

But the road was windy and the headlights were soft and it was so warm. And he wanted to say, Wake me when we get there, but he forgot. And something pulled tight around his neck, around his chest, and all the bags were falling. All the bags were pushing him down.

Everything went quiet and black then.

Until he heard Harry cry.

Until he heard Harry.


Miles opened his eyes and it was dark. It was night-time. He sat up and he could see a figure asleep on a chair next to the bed in the glow of the low grey light coming from the hall. It was Joe. He was still there.

Miles leaned back against the pillow quietly but Joe opened his eyes. He sat up and grabbed the side of the bed.

'Are you OK?' he said, and he turned on the lamp. 'Do you need anything? Are you hungry?'

Miles shook his head. He blinked his eyes against the light.

'You came back,' he said.

Joe nodded. He looked down at his hands and let go of the bed. Miles knew they were shaking.

'The wind was too strong,' he said. 'I couldn't get through the strait. I couldn't leave.'

And Miles knew it was lucky Joe hadn't been lost out there, too. He was lucky.

'It was Dad,' Miles said, and Joe stood up out of the chair.

'I know. It's OK. I know what happened.'

But Miles shook his head. 'No,' he said quietly. 'Uncle Nick was there. He was in the car. I saw him there but I forgot.'

Joe opened his mouth but he didn't speak. He stood for a minute then he sat back down on the edge of the chair, and Miles told him about the crash – what he remembered now.

How when he'd opened his eyes again it was dark and there was no sound. No horn, no headlights. But he could see someone was looking down at him. Someone else was there in the car. Dad.

'He left us there,' Miles said. 'He took Nick away and he didn't come back.'

And Miles remembered waiting in the dark and in the cold, and how he'd called out for Mum over and over but she didn't answer. She never answered. And he was too scared to reach out and touch her. He was too scared to move. And he found a blanket on the floor and wrapped it up tight around Harry. And he tried to stay awake.

*T*hey slept on Joe's boat.

Miles didn't know what was meant to happen now. Granddad's house was empty but they moored in close at Lady Bay and he spent the sunny parts of the day up at the house on the verandah. But he liked the boat, the way it felt. Joe had begun building it when he started his apprenticeship and it had taken a long time. All these years. The wood inside golden and soft. The galley and the workspaces, the small kitchenette and the bunk beds. All wood. All made by Joe. And here it was waiting to leave again.

Miles sat on the bed. Joe was studying a roll of charts at the table, taking notes. He was using a ruler to mark out the path he would take to wherever it was he was going. Marking out the fastest path away from here.

Miles stood up suddenly.

'I'm coming with you,' he said. 'To the house.'

Joe looked across at him, his eyes wide. He put his pencil down, leant his hands against the table.

'OK,' he said.

Miles didn't look at anything on the way in the van. He didn't look out the window at the road or the sky or the trees or the river. He just looked at nothing. At his legs and at the inside of the door. He felt sick.

It was Harry's funeral on Friday. Friday, in the cemetery where Mum was buried. Where Granddad was buried. Lots of people would be there and they would all be crying and they would all be saying how terrible it was. Harry wouldn't want those people there, Aunty Jean and the relatives from town. And Miles didn't want to see them. He didn't want to think about any of those people.

When they pulled up the drive, neither of them moved. They sat in the van for a long time, silent, and Joe's face was still, his eyes tired. Miles watched him stare at the house.

'What do you think happened to him?' he said. 'To Dad?'

Joe shook his head.

'I don't know,' he said, and he blinked his eyes clear. 'I hope he's dead.'

The door wasn't locked and the house was quiet and cold. It smelled of damp. Miles almost expected Dad to be there somehow, sitting in his chair in the gloomy room. Sitting there waiting. But he wasn't. There was no one. And it felt like a long time since anyone had been there. Since it had been a place where people lived. A place where he had lived.

Miles walked over to the framed photograph of Mum on the sideboard and picked it up, took the photo carefully out of the frame.

'Cloudy,' he said.

And he knew he was right, now. He remembered. How Nick had grabbed Mum up and hugged her and how she'd laughed. How she'd pushed him away. And he didn't know what that meant, if it meant something or nothing. But he wanted to keep it, the photo. He wanted to take it with him.

Joe moved close, took the photograph out of his hands. When Miles turned around he could see how much they were the same, Mum and Joe. How much they looked the same. Their eyes and the colour of their hair. Their skin.

'Do I look like her?' Miles asked.

Joe looked down at him and nodded. He handed back the photograph. 'Yes,' he said. 'Yes.'

The bedroom was exactly as it had been. Piled neatly in the corner of the room were Harry's show bags, still half full. Harry was always saving everything.

Miles let the bag he was stuffing with clothes fall to the floor.

'We don't have to get everything now,' Joe said, and he bent down, picked up the bag. 'I'll come back tomorrow, OK?'

Miles sat down on Harry's bed. The doona was cold under his hands and he dug his fists into it.

'I don't want to go to the funeral, Joe. I'm not going. I don't want to see those people, Aunty Jean and relatives I don't even know. I don't want to see them.'

Joe put the bag down on the bed. His voice was soft.

'Stuart will be there – kids from school. And George. You might regret it, not going. Not saying goodbye.'

Miles tried to look at Joe, but his eyes were raw. They wanted to close. There was too much light.

'I'm staying here,' he said, and he felt Joe sit down on the bed.

And he was staying. He was going to stay with Harry. Stay here. Joe didn't understand. He didn't know. Harry might come back, come here. Like Mum. Remember, Harry? How Mum came back? She came back sometimes when we couldn't sleep. I know she did.

'I didn't mean to fall asleep,' he said, and the weight of his body gave way.

But he felt an arm around him. He felt it tight.

'Let's just go, Miles – you and me.'

He listened to Joe talk about all the places they would go, the tropical islands and the clear warm water, the big bright lights of new cities. The free open space of ocean. And he knew that Joe was going to take him with him, now. Wherever he went.

He leant his head down against his brother's shoulder. He let himself cry.

*M*iles stood on the deck of Joe's boat and looked out at the water. His eyes moved over it slowly, carefully. The bay was calm now, still, and it was hard to believe that the swell had ever been so big, that there had ever been a storm. But Miles could see where it had been. What it had touched. Boulders the size of cars had been pushed over so that the shellfish and plants living safely underneath were now stuck metres above the water, exposed to the sun. Hip-high piles of kelp, ripped loose from their roots, blacked out the beach, and whole trees, leaves and all, lay battered and smashed on the rocks.

Joe said it had been the biggest swell he had ever seen. Banks that had been working forever were wiped out – gone. The whole coastline had been changed.

But the bluff was still there, the reef solid. A tiny
swell running on the surface. Tiny ripples turning
into small lines. Little waves beginning to peel,
pulling right and wrapping around the reef. Waves
that could be something as the tide dropped. Waves
that could be working.

Light wind.

Winter sun.

It could be something.

And Miles could feel it in him. The water.

With his board tucked under his arm, his bare feet
hit the sand. And he ran down the beach. The sun
was up high with that bright blinding white coming
right off the water, and out there, the silhouette of a
boy moving – taking to the air, his arms outstretched
like an eagle. And even before Miles paddled up, even
before he could see that face, he knew it was Justin
Roberts. Unmistakable. Justin out there, with his big
mouth and his big teeth saying, Give me another one
of those. Just give me another one and I'll show you
something.

Miles let the rip that ran with the bluff carry him.
He enjoyed the ride, felt his hands slipping through
the cool water, body floating free. And there was this
feeling in him like when it had all just been for fun,
the water. Him and Justin out here on their foamies

all summer – out until dark, ripping on all those shories, ripping the life right out of them, wishing that the sun would stay up just a bit longer. Just one more. Just give me one more.

Mum would be in the Holden waiting and she'd honk the horn.

'Come on, you two – time to go. Time to get dry. It's dark!'

And they'd get in the car with the heater on, and they'd be starving – suddenly starving. They'd drop Justin off. They'd drop Justin home to the stone house over the bluff.

'See you tomorrow.'

'We'll get some good ones tomorrow!'


Justin waved, looked him right in the eye, no fear.

'Long wait between sets, but I thought, stuff it. Not going to get any better today.'

And that was it. Just like always. Talking about the water – talking about the waves.

Miles noticed the board beneath Justin gleaming. No dings, no wax gone brown from grime and sand. Just a clean white surface, brand spanking new.

'Dad got it for me. Have a go if you want.'

Miles didn't waste a second. He found his leg rope and ripped it loose. A new board, light and sharp, and Miles sat tall, let the first wave roll underneath him. He reached his arms to the sky as it bucked.

God. Remember this, Justin? The first time we came out to this reef? The first time we made it out the back? We just decided, looked at those waves and said, Let's go – let's just go. Hearts racing, saying, Yes! Come on, it's time now. Ducking under the white water over and over until we were shaking. Looking out at all that deep water, all that dark water. Being scared. Seeing the face of the reef as the tide rolled back. Sitting where we are right now. Like this.

Right here.

Remember?

When did I forget about this?

Miles and Justin fought for the next line, but Miles was all over it, the board fast and loose under his feet and everything was right.

It felt good. Just like it should.

'You can give me my stick back now,' Justin yelled from behind, but Miles wasn't ready to give this up. Not yet. He'd paddle out for one more. Just one more.

'I'm sorry about your brother,' Justin said, before he walked off, before he walked home. And Miles wanted to say goodbye. To tell Justin thanks for everything, for all of it. But he didn't. He just stood and watched and waved as Justin moved down the beach, wet feet shoved into his sneakers.

He could feel them. Mum and Harry. They were right there behind him, waiting in the Holden – Harry in the front seat grinning and telling him to hurry up. Telling him they were getting fish and chips.

And he wanted them to stay with him a while longer. He wanted them to stay.

He heard the sound of a horn and turned around.

It was Joe.

Joe was waiting for him.

Sometimes in the morning, when the mist hovered in the trees and fog covered the ground and rolled out thick on the water, it meant the winter light would come.

And Miles loved that light.

It made the dark water sparkle, turned the white spray golden – made the ocean a giant mirror reflecting the sky.

Even the leaves on the crack wattle shone in that light.

It made everything come to life.

And they were going to Cloudy. They were leaving.

The water was calm, resting and waiting and letting them pass. Just the right amount of wind to sail without having to work hard, without having to work at all. They moved silently into the bay and through thinning mist, Cloudy looked brand new. Just born, the outlines becoming sharp as the sun rose, as the fog cleared. And like a dream, the waking cliffs glowed orange and the sand lit up silver and the sky, still pale violet, was full and open.

George was there waiting, Jake by his side.

Standing on sand, it seemed that none of them needed to talk. That none of them needed words. They walked together into the dunes to a place where wind couldn't touch and tide would never reach. Joe knelt down and dug a small hole in the damp sandy soil. And they still didn't speak. Even Jake sat quietly.

All the things that Harry had left behind, scattered on the floor and tucked away in drawers and shoved to the back of his cupboard. His show bags full of lollies that he had tried so hard to save, his red plastic skateboard with bearings rusted solid, his old dirty sneakers. They were just things. They were no use anymore.

And when Miles thought about his brother, now, it was the carefully collected shells and rocks, the driftwood and bones that mattered most. Harry's treasure hunt items that had taken up all the windowsills and mantelpieces and verandah space at Granddad's.

Miles had brought the best ones back to Cloudy. The petrified seahorse, the huge cuttlefish cartridge that Harry had carved his name into, and the dried and shrunken Port Jackson shark egg. Although technically Harry hadn't found that one. Not really.

Miles combed the dirty layers of caked wax on his board, making lines to give him grip. Harry had made them late because he didn't want to get in the stupid dinghy, and any minute now the sea breeze would pick up and everything would be wrecked.

'What should I find?' Harry asked.

Joe was shaking his wetsuit out over and over. 'Um . . . A cuttlefish bone, a nice bit of driftwood . . .'

'A shark egg,' Miles said.

It had just come out of his mouth and he didn't want to look up because he knew Joe would be staring right at him. He knew he shouldn't have said it. Harry would look everywhere for a shark egg and he'd never look in the right places. He'd never find one.

'You coming?' said Joe. He was already wading out and Harry had gone. He'd run off down the beach.

Miles looked out to the water. Perfect three-foot glass, empty and waiting and no wind yet. Not yet.

And he couldn't believe he was going to give up clean waves for this, for Harry. But he was going to. He'd already put his board down on the sand.

He watched Harry move into the dunes. God, he wasn't going to find much in there. If there were eggs anywhere they'd be up near Whale Bone Point. The current pushed loose stuff up there. Anything that floated. And it had just been a full moon. There was a chance.

A small chance.

Miles poured a cup of tea into the thermos lid, warmed his hands. He'd stayed out in the water for ages. There had been time after all. Plenty. The water just for him.

'Did you look over there for an egg, Harry?' Miles pointed to the rock pools and gnarled reef that made up Whale Bone Point.

Harry was stuffing his face with a fat slice of Aunty Jean's carrot cake. 'I looked everywhere,' he said, white butter icing stuck to his lips.

'Are you sure you looked over there?'

Harry just stared at him then took another bite of cake. Miles walked over to his towel and pulled the Port Jackson shark egg out from under it. He threw it at Harry. It landed on the sand right near his feet and Harry looked at it for a long time. He didn't even chew.

'Is the shark out of it?' he said, finally.

Miles nodded. The brown covering of the egg had spiralled open, its contents long gone.

'But I didn't find it.'

'You would have if you'd looked over there properly.'

Harry put the remaining bit of cake down. He touched the egg with his fingers, held it up to the light.

Yes, he nodded.

'Thanks,' he said.


Joe was touching his arm. The sun had moved in the sky and time had run on. Time had gotten away.

Miles bent down and put the shark egg in the hole. He put the seahorse in, too, but kept the cuttlefish tight in his hand. He'd hang on to it. He'd take it with them. Just one thing.

Joe filled the hole. He patted it solid and marked the spot with shells they had collected on the way through to the dunes. Old shells, white and ancient. Shells that had been at Cloudy forever.

It was time to go.

Joe shook George's hand goodbye and when Miles

went to do the same, George grabbed him up quick, pulled him in tight.

'Don't look back,' he said in his way so that all the words ran together. But Miles understood. And he knew he wouldn't come back here, not for a long time. Then George put something in his hand. Something small and cold, sharp against his skin.

The white pointer's tooth, come back to him.

And in his mind he saw Uncle Nick get in the car. He leant over and stroked Harry's cheek. He looked at Miles.

'This is for you,' he said, and he put the tooth in his hands.

'For luck.'

Miles looked up at George, his eyes full of tears.

'You found him,' he said. 'Harry.'

And George nodded. 'Yes,' he said softly.

Jake barked, and George waved goodbye as they set off in the dinghy and headed out to the boat. Miles looked back down the curved wide beach of Cloudy one last time. Out of all the places, all the cliffs and rocks and black water and good waves rushing, this place was the only one he would miss. Cloudy was special, always brighter, and Harry was free to stay here now. Free to run along this beach until the end of time.

Out past the shallows, past the sandy-bottomed bays, comes the dark water – black and cold and roaring. Rolling out an invisible path, a new line for them to follow.

To somewhere warm.
To somewhere new.

# Acknowledgements

I would like to warmly thank the following people – Vanessa Radnidge for believing in this book and working so hard to get it across the line. I will never forget all that you have done for me; Janey Runci for the years of encouragement and inspiration. I owe much of this book to your incredible teaching; The Queensland Writers Centre; the Australian Society of Authors; Julia Stiles and Roberta Ivers; Fiona Hazard, Kate Ballard, Laura Drewe, Matt Richell, Louisa Dear, Clare Meldrum, Emily Brannan, Brendan Fredericks, Heather Young, Dannielle Williams, Jodie Mann, Daniel Pilkington and the Hachette team; David Kneale; James, Chiyoko and Haruki Parrett; Mum and Steve; Amanda Graham; Kim Bear; Robyn

Bunting and Max; Edwinda Shaw; Jacinda Pfeffer; Fotina, Kathryn and Siobahn; Angela Slatter; the Joondo 8; the music of Gareth Edwards; and lastly, all the great writers in my writing groups (past and present) who have helped me along the way.

# Reading Group Guide

## About the Book

*Past the Shallows* is a hauntingly beautiful story of the bond of brotherhood and the fragility of youth.

Told with an elegant simplicity, this is the story of two brothers growing up in a fractured family on the wild Tasmanian coast. The consequences of their parents' choices shape their lives and ultimately bring tragedy to them all.

Harry and Miles live with their father, an abalone fisherman, on the south-east coast of Tasmania. With their mum dead, they are left to look after themselves. When Miles isn't helping out on the boat they explore the coast and Miles and his older brother, Joe, love to surf. Harry is afraid of the water.

Every day their dad battles the unpredictable ocean to make a living. He is a hard man, a bitter drinker who harbours a devastating secret that is destroying him. Unlike Joe, Harry and Miles are too young to leave home and so are forced to live under the dark cloud of their father's mood, trying to stay as invisible as possible whenever he is home. Harry, the youngest, is the most vulnerable and it seems he bears the brunt of his father's anger.

## Review Raves

'Parrett's writing has a real voice, with power to evoke feeling, place and character. She is capable of refreshing narrative clarity, yet at other times surprises with an intense lyricism that is never self-indulgent. Everyone is put to the test, pushed to the edge physically and spiritually in a series of events and revelations that affect not only the characters but also the reader. This book is that rare thing, a finely crafted literary novel that is genuinely moving and full of heart.' *The Age*

'an extraordinary debut novel, part psychological family drama. Part mystery, part painful rite of passage, engulfed in the wild isolation and natural richness of the Tasmanian coast. Favel Parrett's intimate understanding of this rugged heel of the world seeps through every pore of this book, especially her descriptions of the water, so vivid you can feel the chill and rush of the waves, the pull of the undertow and the ominous danger of the deep . . . Touching and quite beautiful, Favel Parrett is a fresh and vital new voice in Australian fiction.' *Australian Women's Weekly*

'*Past the Shallows* reminds me of other Australian novels, such as those of Tim Winton, focused on our relationship with the unforgiving seas that surround us, and the wild landscapes in which we live . . . It is an impressive first book, with exquisite imagery and poetic writing' *Courier-Mail*

'*Past the Shallows* spins a beautiful and shining web of a cruelly dysfunctional family set on the rugged southern coast of Tasmania . . . This is one of the most powerful and moving books this reviewer has read. *Past the Shallows*, an amazing book by a wonderful writer – Cormac McCarthy meets David Vann meets Favel Parrett. Read this book.' *Sunday Times*

'One of Parrett's great achievements is the way she captures the children's voices: these narrators are, unquestionably, children rather than adult ventriloquists . . . *Past the Shallows* is an even, thoughtful book and clearly the work of a talented new novelist.' *Weekend Australian*

'Parrett has crafted a small gem of a story, haunting and alive . . . the beauty of the writing uplifts the reader.' *Who Weekly*

'Parrett . . . has created truly believable characters and her prose's as powerful as a rip.' *The Australian*

'Favel Parrett's debut novel, *Past the Shallows*, marks the addition of a  strong voice to the chorus of Australian literature.' *Canberra Times*

'*Past the Shallows* will remind readers of Tim Winton, both in its concerns and in its evocation of wild places. Parrett's prose captures the Tasmanian coastline and weather in all its splendour and unpredictability, and yet in its deceptive simplicity will not be beyond the reach of the younger reader. Like Winton's *That Eye, The Sky*, Parrett's debut is an uncompromising and memorable tale.' *Sunday Tasmanian*

## An Interview with Favel Parrett

with Tanya Caunce for tlcbooks.wordpress.com

**Can you introduce yourself to the readers; what would you like them to know about you?**
My name is Favel. A strange name I know, one that I hated when I was young but have come to like very much. I was always told there was an old English legend about a horse called Favel that you could brush and ask for favours. I do not know if it is exactly true, but in the way stories wrap around us, it has become part of my story.

I grew up in Tasmania, but have lived in Victoria for a long time now. Victoria is home.

**Have you always wanted to be a writer or do you have an equal or greater passion for something else?**
I always wanted to be a writer but I never thought it would be possible. When I first seriously sat down and started this novel, I knew in my heart that I *really* did want to be a writer. I still thought it would be impossible, but I kept going anyway.

I have done many things – been a postman, a DJ, worked in a bakery, failed at finishing my degree at university, travelled to lots of wonderful places like Bhutan and Zambia and Cuba and Kenya. I am passionate about many things. I am probably the most passionate about dogs! When I have time I volunteer at an animal rescue shelter called Pets Haven. They save so many lives every year. It is a place that means the world to me.

**_Past the Shallows_ is your debut published novel, but is it your first novel?**
It is my first novel. I never thought I could actually write a novel but somehow I did (over many years). I wrote before, short stories mainly – some published, most not. In my late teens and early twenties, I published a ZINE called _Numb_ (homemade, photo-copied, cut-and-paste magazine full of rants and opinions and all sorts of stuff). I was a huge ZINE fan and I met so many great people. It was before email, so there was lots of letter writing. I used to get so excited checking my mailbox after work. That doesn't happen much these days. I miss it!

**Who are the authors you most admire?**
This list gets longer every day, but here are just a few . . .

Maya Angelou – She taught me about the power of words, the power of writing with truth. I love her.

Per Petterson – *Out Stealing Horses* is one of the best books I have ever read. I read it often. He is a master. I have learnt so much from his writing.

Cormac McCarthy – *The Road* is an incredible book. We are so with the characters that we cannot pull away, even when we want to. Even when we don't want to be on that road anymore. The last paragraph is up on my wall in my studio and I read it most days. It still moves me as much as it did the first time I read it.

I love novels. All the care and time and heart that goes into them. Some novels have changed my life. I know they are important.

**Where is your favourite place to write?**
**(not necessarily the best . . .)**
I spend half my week in Torquay and half in Melbourne. I write in both places but I do my best work in my studio in the Nicholas building on Swanston Street. It is filled with other artists and galleries and has two old cage lifts with lift operators that are always up for a chat. It is a great place to work. It is my office!

**What was the inspiration for *Past the Shallows*?**
The south coast of Tasmania had a huge influence on me when I was young. It is isolated and wild – a place I will never forget. The story grew out of my memories and feeling for that place. It is a sad and beautiful place. An ancient place.

**How did you come up with the title?**
The title came from the first line of the book: 'Out past the shallows, past the sandy-bottomed bays, comes the dark water – black and cold and roaring.' It was actually my publishers' brilliant idea. For a long time, I knew the book as Crack Wattle. I knew this title wasn't quite right, but it did mean something to me. There is still a section in the book about crack wattle. Then, when they suggested changing it to Past the Shallows I knew it was perfect straight away. I think it is a great title.

**Which character spoke the loudest, to you? Did any of them clamour to be heard over the others?**
I love Harry very much. Sometimes it still makes me cry when I think about him. He is a very special character to me – some kind of gift really.

Although Harry is not totally based on my brother, the way I feel about my brother is there in the writing.

One of the worst things that could have happened to me when I was a child would have been losing my brother. We are very close.

**The ocean and its guises feature heavily in the book, like a character of its own. What is your connection with the ocean?**

You are right. The ocean is a character of its own. I am in love with the Southern Ocean. I know that surfing changed my life. I'm thirty-six and I still love it. It connected me to the natural world, made me aware of tides and winds and the subtle changes that happen every minute of every day. I couldn't have written this book if I did not surf. And I know I am grumpy and hopeless if I go for more than a week without getting in the water. My favourite time to surf is at dawn, watching the sun come up over Torquay and illuminate the cliffs and sand with the new day.

**I know you are working on your next book. Can you share a bit about it?**

I will give you a bit of a blurb, although I don't know the whole story yet. The working title is 'Time of the Vikings'.

A young girl and her brother try to find their way in a new place. A stone city full of ghosts and empty streets. A place where the wind blows in cold and from the south.

Everything gets brighter when the Vikings come to town – the men who work on an Antarctic supply vessel from Denmark. They are giants and they breathe life into Hobart. Chasing the light from the Arctic to the Antarctic, they sail the world end to end, never stopping for long enough for the darkness to catch them.

But there is a terrible accident off Macquarie Island.

And nothing is ever the same.

## Suggested Discussion Points

- Aunty Jean is the only female role model the boys have left. She is at times cruel and caring towards them. Do you consider her a good person? Do you have any sympathy for her? What references within the text have led you to this opinion?

- Do you think George Fuller sees Harry as just another puppy to rescue? Or does he genuinely care for Harry? There are a few other works of literature that use an ostracised figure in the community to enhance our understanding of the main characters. Why do you think this can be a useful plot device, and do you think it's effective here?

- This is a small community where everyone knows who everyone is, as we can see from Mr Roberts, George and Mrs Martin in the store. In light of this, why do you think the boys' home life is allowed to continue? What is the role of men in this community?

- There're few female figures in Harry's and Miles's lives. Is there any evidence of what they think about women?

- What would be some of the challenges of living here?

- How challenging would it be to be a woman in this community?

- Jeff exhibits increasingly dangerous and bullying behaviour: the staring, shooting the shark and risking hitting Miles, forcing Harry to drink. Does he bring about Dad's worst behaviour to his sons? Or do you think Dad allows Jeff free rein to reveal his ugly nature? Do you have any sympathy for Dad? What is the evidence within the text that formed your opinion?

- 'Harry stood there looking at the tooth in his hands, and he looked so young and small like no time had ever passed by since he was the baby in the room and Joe had told Miles to be nice to him and help Mum out. And Miles had thought he wouldn't like it. But Harry had a way about him. A way that made you promise to take care of him.' (page 199)

Both Joe and Miles are forced to take on responsibility for their brothers, yet they do it quite differently. Joe moved out with Granddad and left the other two behind with their dad when he was thirteen and then ultimately leaves the two of them forever. Miles however stays on even after he is beaten by his father. Why do you think they approach the responsibility so differently?

- Miles and Harry share an unbreakable bond. Discuss their different reactions to Joe leaving.

- Joe is also part of this family unit. Why do you think he is painted as one of the family, but also an outsider? He used to work on the boat, now doesn't. He moved to live with his grandfather. Why do you think Favel Parrett chose not to include point of view from Joe? What effect does this have on the novel? What do you imagine his story would have been?

- The water throughout the novel is a metaphor for Dad. Do you agree or not, and what from the text made you think this way? Harry fears the water and Miles both loves and hates it. Is there anything within the book that shows us how this relates to the boys' relationship with Dad?

- 'There was something coming.

    Miles had felt it in the water. Seen it. Swell coming in steady, the wind right on it, pushing. It was ground swell. Brand new and full of punch – days away from its peak.' (page 185)

    How does the Tasmanian landscape speak for the character's emotions within the text? Are there other references to nature within the book that you found moving? Discuss.

- Discuss the significance of the shark tooth necklace.

- Memory plays a big part in this novel. Discuss the way in which memories are invoked in *Past the Shallows* and what part they play in the story.

- The gradual piecing together of Miles's memories about his mother and the night of the accident have a sense of fantasy or dream-like state about them. Do you think these events happened chronologically? What makes you think that? Did they reveal events the way you'd imagined? What other possibilities had you anticipated?

- Why do you think Joe wasn't in the car?

- Do you think Harry isn't Dad's son, and Miles and Joe are? Is it clear-cut? What references within the text have given you that impression?

- It's obviously a point of rage for Dad. Do you have any sympathy for him? How did you feel when you learned through Joe that he'd disappeared and there would be no direct confrontation or punishment for his acts? Was this a satisfactory ending for you? Why/why not?

- 'Harry's feet hardly seemed to touch the ground as he followed Jake, and it was easy to run. He ran through the trees, reached out, and he could almost touch Jake's red fur. George was up ahead. George, waving from the top of the hill.

  'And when Harry got there, he could see it all.

  'The land just as it had been forever – untouched.' (page 223)

  Do you believe this is a utopian afterlife image from Harry after death? Or do you think this is a fragment of unconscious dreaming from Miles? How did you reach this conclusion? Are there any other references within the text that have influenced this idea?

• Harry and Miles's story is bookended between the evocative phrase: 'Out past the shallows, past the sandy-bottomed bays, comes the dark water – black and cold and roaring. Rolling out the invisible paths...' What effect did the imagery and repetition have on you going into the beginning of the story? And on leaving the story?

• Although very evocative of the Tasmanian coast, do you think that the story transcends borders, and would be just as thought-provoking to a reader in another country?

## Further Reading

• *Breath* by **Tim Winton**
• *When God was a Rabbit* by **Sarah Winman**
• *Jasper Jones* by **Craig Silvey**
• *Brothers and Sisters* edited by **Charlotte Wood**

*Read more . . .*

Alexander Maksik

**YOU DESERVE NOTHING**

**A dark, compelling story of an illicit affair between a young teacher and his female student**

Set in Paris at an international high school catering to the sons and daughters of wealthy, influential families, *You Deserve Nothing* is a gripping story of power, idealism and morality. It is a thrilling account of what happens when the boundaries that separate teachers and students are crossed.

'This is a hugely satisfying and thought-provoking novel . . . There are echoes of *The Secret History* but *You Deserve Nothing* may be even more immediately appealing' *Daily Mail*

'*You Deserve Nothing* . . . reminds the reader how powerful ideas and literature can be – not just by creating a memorably complex character in Will, but with some stunning prose of its own as well' *Independent on Sunday*

'Rivetingly plotted and beautifully written' *New York Times*

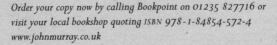
*Order your copy now by calling Bookpoint on 01235 827716 or visit your local bookshop quoting* ISBN *978-1-84854-572-4*
*www.johnmurray.co.uk*

# Read more . . .

## Lloyd Jones

### MISTER PIP

**Shortlisted for the Man Booker Prize**

**Winner of the Commonwealth Writers' Prize**

On a lush island in the South Pacific, civil war threatens daily life. Thirteen-year-old Matilda and her friends haven't seen the inside of a classroom for months until the village recluse emerges to breathe life back into an old book. Surrounded by the constant threat of violence, their new teacher introduces the children to a boy named Pip and a man called Mr Dickens. But on an island at war, the power of stories can have deadly consequences.


'Haunting and morally complex' *Sunday Times*

'A brilliantly nuanced examination of the power of imagination' *Financial Times*

'One of the best books of the year!' Isabel Allende

*Order your copy now by calling Bookpoint on 01235 827716 or visit your local bookshop quoting ISBN 978-0-7195-6994-4 www.johnmurray.co.uk*

## From Byron, Austen and Darwin

to some of the most acclaimed and original contemporary writing, John Murray takes pride in bringing you powerful, prizewinning, absorbing and provocative books that will entertain you today and become the classics of tomorrow.

We put a lot of time and passion into what we publish and how we publish it, and we'd like to hear what you think.

Be part of John Murray – share your views with us at:

www.johnmurray.co.uk

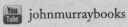 johnmurraybooks

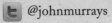 @johnmurrays

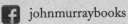 johnmurraybooks